The SCOT'S RECKONING

HIGHLAND HUNTERS 7

KEIRA MONTCLAIR

CHAPTER ONE

Scotland, Early Spring, 1316

THEA DOUGLAS'S HEART broke in two. She didn't know what to do. Why was she always faced with choices—ones that confused her more than ever?

She glanced from one set of beloved people to the other.

On one side of her stood Maitland and Dyna, waiting patiently for her to join their patrol. On the other side? Her parents. Donnan and Bethia Douglas stood side-by-side, both looking more dejected than she'd ever seen them. And her wee sister Lorana held on to her mother's skirt, her mouth with a familiar downward turn.

Her mother said, "I fear ye are still not thinking clearly, Thea."

She had no idea why her mother would say such a thing, other than using it as a trick to keep her home. It was time for her to take a stand and fight for Scotland. She needed to go but didn't know how to convince her parents of her sudden desire to go out in the world. It had come over her recently, this confusion over who she was and where she belonged. Like many of her cousins, she believed the answer could be found out on patrol, protecting fellow Scots from the English. Many of them had found not only themselves but their soulmates, falling in love and marrying soon after.

Shouldn't she be next?

But was marriage the answer? She had no idea. She adored her family, her pets, and her clan, but where did Thea Douglas belong? What was her purpose in the world? Did she have one or was she destined to become her greatest fear?

Nothing special.

"I think I should go," Thea said, looking at her parents so intently that she hoped to block Lorana's face from her view. She hated to disappoint her dear sister.

Maitland said, "We could really use her help. With Ysenda and Isla still on Black Isle, we only have Wenna and possibly Reyna for a short time. What if we agreed to have her check back every fortnight?"

"We could do that," Dyna added.

The duo were on patrol, looking for any Englishmen who didn't belong. King Edward II wanted to take over all of Scotland, but King Robert the Bruce kept him from doing so. King Robert had been assisting his brother in Ireland and had asked Maitland and Dyna to help protect Scotland while he was away. Any Englishmen in the Highlands were up to no good. But their patrol was also to travel into the Lowlands, just to make sure the English weren't gathering forces for an invasion. Edward's men still controlled Berwick Castle, although King Robert vowed to win it back.

Thea's mother looked at her father, and he gave her a subtle nod. Her mother stepped forward and said, "I'd like to have a short chat with my daughter before she takes her leave."

"Of course," Maitland said. "We can visit Ramsay Hall while ye chat with her. We'll check to see if Reyna and Wulf will be joining us. Come to the hall when ye are ready, Thea."

Maitland and Dyna took their leave, and Thea's father said, "Bethia, I can live with every fortnight. Can ye?"

Her mother teared up, but said, "I can too. But Thea, please walk with me."

She nodded, excited that they were allowing her to go. "Mama, I am six and twenty."

"I know ye are. And I know ye can just walk away and we canno' stop ye." Her mother led her out the door and down toward her father's bathing contraption, one of the things Thea missed when she traveled. The feeling of water sluicing over her body could only be duplicated by a fine waterfall in the summer. Her father had managed to find a way to heat the water by the sun, and she loved it. In fact, she and Lorana often showered together, her sister giggling all the while the water fell over them.

She would miss Lorana most of all, even though she was but eight summers.

But she also needed to find herself.

"Go with our blessing, daughter, because I wish to have ye focus well on patrol. I know Scotland needs strong archers to keep our country safe. But I worry about ye, and if ye come back every fortnight, I would no' worry overmuch."

"I understand, Mama. Besides, then I could wash under a nice shower every fortnight." She reached for her mother's hand and smiled. "I need to go, to find out where I belong. Mayhap leaving home will help me find my path."

"I know ye are confused, but ye are so skilled with animals, gentle but thorough, that I had always dreamed ye would stay on Ramsay land and continue my work. My hands may not be able to function for much longer. Ye know how they pain me at night. Or ye could learn from Grandmama and be a healer. Ye have many choices close to home."

Thea knew that, but how did she tell her mother that she wished for something different? She had this driving need to leave their land, to run and feel free. She'd watched her cousins go on patrol, risk their lives, fall in love and become so happy that it had surprised her. Thea hadn't expected to see Reyna or Isla so pleased with their new life. But they were. And Ceit had married Brin Cameron, and now Ysenda had become betrothed to Lewis Haggert.

But she also knew a husband was not the only missing link in her life. She was restless. More than anything, she wished to get away, to travel. See Edinburgh and Glasgow and Ayr. Travel again to Berwick or Inverness. See the busy life in the cities she'd found so intriguing.

Thea was searching for something, and she was certain she'd never find it here on Ramsay land. The last year of her life had been unsettling and dissatisfying, though she wasn't quite sure why. She had an inherent obligation to stay with her parents, but another part of her wished to run free. Which was more powerful at the moment? The second one and she would listen to her gut.

"I promise to be careful, Mama, and I'll be home every fortnight. Ye still have the Ramsay animals to keep ye busy. Promise ye will take care of my dogs. I do hate to leave them, but they have all of ye to take care of them."

Her mother actually rolled her eyes. "'Tis true, but they are never as happy when ye are gone. I'll send them with Torrian and his group for a few days. That should tire them while they wait for ye."

Thea gave her mother a swift hug and kissed her cheek. "I love ye, Mama. Drystan will return for a visit soon. I'm sure he's due." Her only brother was spending several moons training with Connor Grant, renowned for his sword skills. He joked that he was fostering at the advanced age of four and thirty.

"All right," her mother said, staring off into the trees as if considering her words carefully. "Go with my blessing. Keep yer eyes focused and get yer rest. Listen to Maitland and Dyna. They know battle conditions well. I hope King Robert will return to fight soon. We need to end Edward's constant attacks." Her mother kissed her cheek and gave her a swift hug. "Go pack yer bags, and I'll prepare a food sack for ye."

Thea whistled for her deerhounds, Bo and Gerland. The two dogs came racing across the landscape from the woods, their favorite playground. The brothers were still young, two-year-old littermates from Torrian's best pair of hounds. They still acted like wee pranksters, despite their large size.

Bo was the darker of the two, and his haunches wiggled all the while his tail wagged. He loved to brush up against her when he was extra excited. The brief feeling of guilt for leaving them that washed over her would not change her mind.

"Ye willnae be so excited when ye realize I'm gone. Just for a short time, then I'll be back."

Gerland was a wee bit taller and a lighter gray. His nose pushed her hand looking for a treat or an ear rub.

"I have no treats, only ear rubs for ye." She aggressively petted both dogs while they wiggled and made odd sounds of pleasure. "Ye must stay here and protect Lorana."

Her father came out of the cottage and the two headed for him at full speed. "Good. Da, will ye distract them for a wee bit? I must go pack."

Her father didn't speak much, but his few words were usually invaluable. "Yer mother still worries about ye. Dinnae disappoint her." His hair was a mix of gray and dark brown. His face bore the wrinkles that showed his age, but his hands were as nimble as ever. Aunt Brenna had claimed it was because he kept them working so much with all his gadgets and inventions.

Thea adored him. He was her rock, always there for her with words of sage advice, which she treasured and tucked away. She would miss him dearly, as she would her mother and sister.

"I know," she said, standing on her tiptoes to kiss his cheek. "But Drystan should return soon."

"Ye know what I mean, lass."

Rather than listen to any more lecturing, she decided to take her leave. "I must go pack, Papa."

"Godspeed to ye, and we'll see ye in a fortnight, no later." He nodded his head for emphasis then headed out to his hut full of wood and tools. He had built the shop years ago to give him the room to create all his contraptions, and she usually loved to go with him, but not today.

Thea was going on an adventure, and she couldn't wait to see what it would bring.

Willum MacLerie sat in the middle of the Ramsay great hall, waiting for Maitland and Dyna to arrive so they could update him on their next patrol. His parents had come to spend Yule with his mother's family, only to find out that Grandda and Grandmama were on Black Isle.

Aunt Sorcha sat down next to him. "Are ye anxious to leave, Willum? I think Cadyn may decide to go on the next patrol."

Willum nodded. "Ye know I like to keep moving, Auntie. I hope Cadyn will join us again soon. Is there a reason he's not going on this patrol with us?" He knew Cadyn was newly married but hadn't expected it to change his life entirely, though all the recent match ups between patrol members seemed to have changed many of their lives. He couldn't help but wonder when his turn would come to find the love of his life.

"Tryana is carrying, and she's having a difficult time with the bairn. And Perrin is also struggling with his new life, though he's much happier here than he was in his previous location. Wulf and Tryana are doing their best to meet all his needs. But the poor lad panics whenever anyone mentions leaving Ramsay land. So having Cadyn leave for patrol would be devastating for him. He's become quite attached to him."

"I wish him well, but please tell him he is missed."

"I will. Now 'tis yer turn to find a wife. Have ye looked or considered anyone?"

Surprised his aunt had come so close to reading his mind, he blushed. "I have time."

"And Wenna. She should find someone soon. She is older than ye by a few years. Is that no' true, Willum?"

"Aye. She is seven and twenty. I am two years younger. Neither of us are in any hurry."

"I'm going to find Cailean. Godspeed to ye on this trip."

Aunt Sorcha took her leave just as the door opened. Maitland and Dyna came in the door, and Maitland headed straight to Willum's table while Dyna headed to his parents, seated at a different table.

"Ye are ready, Willum?"

"Aye. Just give me an hour's notice." He glanced over at his father and nodded to let him know he was indeed leaving. His mother wished to wait for her parents to return, so they'd be staying on for another sennight at least.

"Excellent," Maitland said. "We have received a request for a short assignment. King Robert wishes for us to travel toward Edinburgh. He's learned of a small band of Englishmen who are attacking traveling Scots somewhere between here and the city, stealing any coin they have. Our king thinks they are based in Edinburgh. We'll no' need a large group for this one."

Willum's father stood and joined them. "Maitland, I'm guessing ye are gathering a group for another patrol for King Robert?"

Maitland clasped the older man's shoulder. "Aye, I'd like Willum to join us on this patrol, Will. We plan to return in a fortnight, and then I'd like Wenna to join us for the next journey. This one should be a short trip, so we dinnae need many. I'm no' sure about the next patrol, but I like to be prepared ahead of time."

"Who are the six for this trip?" Will asked.

"Thea, Willum, Reyna, and Wulf," he replied, knowing it was understood that Dyna was also traveling.

His father glanced at him with a subtle smile. "I'm sure Willum is anxious to go along. He doesn't stay in one place for long, as ye know, Maitland. Willum, take one of the falcons with ye, if ye'd like."

"They are always welcome," Maitland replied with a smile.

Willum was pleased with the list of travelers and with the chance to take a falcon along. Even more, he was anxious for the conversation to end so he could leave the hall and prepare for their journey. He hated crowds, especially inside. He preferred to see just trees and the sky over his head at night when he fell asleep.

His parents had started to raise him and his sister in a cave, and now it was difficult for him to be inside for long periods. After many years, they had eventually moved to a small cottage not far from Ramsay land, but he preferred the sky to be his roof in the summer and autumn. Many times he'd slept behind their cottage in the warm months. The peacefulness of the birds and the fresh air settled his soul. But he'd also spent many nights in a deep cave, a fire near the mouth keeping them warm at night. His mother had made some of their clothing from the skins of rabbits and deer simply because they stayed warmer and drier. She had a special skill in working leather and pelts, and she brought several new items for her family for Yule.

He had stood when Aunt Sorcha took her leave and his father joined them, in part out of respect but also because he couldn't wait to head out that door, even if the skies were gray and cloudy. When he spent too long inside, his skin dried to a texture he hated, simply because of the hearth.

But his patience had paid off. Now that he knew Thea was coming along, the journey was even more inviting. If he could just sneak away to chat with her, he'd be even happier.

He had to admit that the more he saw of Thea Douglas, the more he liked her. She was a powerful archer, and that made her a powerful woman. Smart and pretty, she was also one of the few from the clan who was a little wider in the hip than most. That pleased him. Though he'd spent most of his life living in the wilderness and a cave, he'd been with enough women to know that he preferred them not to be thin. He was tall like his father, and the one time he'd been with a thin woman, he'd feared he'd hurt her every time he touched her.

Thea was near perfection in his eyes. Strong, smart, skilled, and clever. Solid. That's what he'd call her. What more could he want in a woman? Not the kind of woman to be blown away by the wind. Poor Ysenda had been tossed over the side of a ravine like she was naught more than a twig, bouncing and breaking along the way. Had she been built more like Thea, she never would have had the injuries she'd had, he'd wager.

His sister Wenna was thin too. Even though she was older than him, she had much to learn yet. She'd struggled with archery but had kept at it because their mother had been one of the finest archers in all the land. She could finally handle her bow well, and rode a fine horse, but her attention often flitted when in the wilderness. She had an intense fear of spiders and boar. All it took was one spider to drop on her arm from a treetop and her screams could be heard from afar.

"Wenna is staying back?" he asked his father.

"Aye, she wished to see her grandparents before she goes. I'm sure ye'll see them when ye return, but she likes to spend time with Grandmama out on the archery field, cold weather and all." His father ran his hand through his hair, pulling a few of the wild strands away from his face. "We hate to disappoint her since we are here."

The door opened, and Thea strode in, tossing a bag off to the side. She headed straight for their table.

"It didnae take ye long to pack," Maitland said.

"Nay, I'm ready to travel again." She grinned and waggled her brow at Willum. "Ye know I love to move about."

That look sent his mind to thoughts he'd never admit, the waggle of her brow a seductive look that went straight to his privates. The expression on her face conjured visions of Thea on horseback, fighting the enemy with a fierce glare. He loved to watch her. Her ability to focus on her mark was impressive, something most warriors had to learn over years of practice, if he were to guess. Thea had that ability as though it had been born inside her, like the animals of the forest, patient in their stalking. She was the queen of the creatures, a vision that he found so alluring and enticing, he had to force himself to calm down and slow his heartbeat.

He glanced around at the others in the hall, which he knew would quell his body, but his reaction to her presence gave him pause. He had to learn how to control his carnal reaction to this woman.

Or they could both be in trouble on patrol.

CHAPTER TWO

T HEA GLANCED UP at Willum, the most
  mysterious member of their patrols, his long
dark hair often hiding his features in the wind.
He spoke little, but he noticed everything.

"Thea, I'm bringing a falcon along on this trip.
Would ye care to join me as I get him ready?"

"Aye, I'd be happy to."

"I'll carry yer bag out for ye."

Thea nearly swooned at this small gesture.
While normally she'd be upset at the offer of
help—she was perfectly capable of carrying her
own bag—she liked the idea of a man helping
her out, especially Willum.

She had a suspicion why many of her cousins
had fallen for a man on patrol. It was the freedom
from the clan. She was free from her parents or
Uncle Logan looking over her shoulder ready
to tell all. Since she hadn't traveled much in her
life, she knew few others besides the Ramsay and
Grant men, and she was related to most of them.

Brenna Grant marrying Quade Ramsay made
a wonderful alliance between the two clans, but

it made marriage of all their descendants difficult because Brenna would not allow any cousins to marry.

However, many youngsters had been adopted into both clans, so those people could easily marry anyone without concern. Aunt Molly, Aunt Maggie, Loki, Simone, Kenzie, and so many others had been adopted. Willum was one of these; his mother, born in England, had been adopted.

But a far more important point was that Willum was handsome. He was the silent, enigmatic type who managed his sword as well as his bow, but was gentle enough to handle any type of bird or animal without a feather out of place. She and Willum had that much in common. He seemed more comfortable around animals than people, as she often did. Her mother took care of the animals in the clan—cows, sheep, horses, dogs, chickens—all of them. Though her mother didn't have as much experience with birds, Thea was drawn to the feathered friends as much as any animal. And since Thea spent many of her days with her mother, she handled animals and birds nearly as well as her teacher.

So did Willum. And she liked seeing a tall, dark-haired man reach for a rabbit and pet it like it was the finest thing in the world. She swore he cooed to one once. She'd giggled, and he'd cast a sweet grin her way.

Therefore, she felt no guilt when she swooned for the first time in her life as he picked up her bag, held the door for her, then moved ahead of her and glanced back with a waggling brow and a smile.

Especially since his eyes were the oddest mix of blue and green. She'd heard the deepest waters in the world were that color, but she had no idea. All she knew was she preferred those mystical eyes to be on her.

"Which falcon are ye bringing along?" she asked, running to keep up with his long strides.

"My choice is the peregrine. They have the absolute fastest dive of any bird, and watching them is a treat. His name is Blue because his eyes are nearly blue instead of the usual blue-gray. I've had him about three years." He led her down to the area outside the gate, then whistled and held his arm up, the heavy wool of his tunic protection against the bird's talons. It appeared that someone had sewn an extra thick patch of material on the arm of his garment for just this purpose.

Almost immediately, a swift, slim bird of prey appeared. Thea had heard about falconry mostly because of Willum's father, who was renowned as a trainer. In fact, he'd trained birds for the current king's father, Edward I, once.

The current King Edward would never request such a thing—the hateful bastard. She found falconry fascinating but had never had an opportunity to try it. Perhaps she could learn about it from Willum. It would give her the chance to spend more time with him.

The falcon circled overhead, and as soon as Willum let out a second whistle, it locked its eyes on its trainer and headed for him, executing a beautiful swoop before diving toward Willum. Thea took two steps back as the bird spread its wings to slow its descent.

"Dinnae be afraid. I promise ye if ye stood close, Blue would make sure no' to hit ye with his wings. They have amazing control." His face lit up as Blue moved closer, and Thea was caught between watching the enjoyment on Willum's face and the exhilaration of the bird's flight. Willum reached for her with his other hand, stilling her as he cooed to his pet, who landed in an instant, flapping its wings, much like the wave of a king's arms who had just bestowed an award on the finest knight. The falcon was so majestic, with the gray and black head against the white throat. She was mesmerized by its skill and power.

Once the bird landed, Willum offered it a small treat, and the bird accepted it before turning to assess her as it ate.

"Would ye like to have him land on yer arm?" Willum asked, his expression quite serious. He felt her sleeve, and said, "Plenty thick enough. He'll no' hurt yer tender skin, I promise."

"But would he no' prefer to perch on yer arm than mine?" She had to admit she was a wee bit apprehensive about the prospect of those sharp talons hitting her skin.

"Nay. I'll stand here next to ye. Aye? Give it a try?"

She nodded, but mostly because she was captivated by his eyes up close. The sun came out at that moment, making his eyes look the color of a clear summer sky, except with sparkles.

"What's wrong?"

"Naught," she said, swallowing hard because she'd been caught staring. "Yer eyes are such an odd shade. Part blue and part green. What a beautiful color."

"Like my sire. His are the same. Wenna's are blue like Mama's. But what say ye? Will ye allow Blue to land on yer arm?" He leaned down to whisper in her ear. "I promise ye that ye will enjoy it."

Shivers shot up her spine, leaving her suddenly powerless to reject him. She was so enthralled from standing this close to Willum that she nodded without thinking of the consequences. The man had her spellbound. Why had she never noticed him like this before?

The man affected her more than any other ever had. When had a man ever caused her to forget what she'd been thinking about? Too many questions with no answers. Her heart was overpowering her mind.

Willum raised his arm and swung it to the side just a touch, and Blue sailed off into the sky, then swooped down before flying higher again.

"What do I do?" Her gaze darted back and forth between Willum and Blue. What had she been thinking to agree to this? She had no idea how to stay calm, and she'd had enough experience with animals to know how important one's demeanor was in order to gain their trust. The consequences of ignoring this simple code could be disastrous.

He turned his body and wrapped his arm around her shoulders. "Relax and ye'll be fine. Just listen. I'll whistle for him. He'll not listen to ye. Did ye know that some of the kings of old would train their falcons to shade them from the sun? Of course, we are cloudy so often that we dinnae truly need it, but I've often wondered how to train a bird to do such a thing. A falcon or a hawk they would use for shade. Could ye imagine?"

"That sounds verra interesting. I would love to hear more about how ye train them. But I'm a wee bit nervous. Will ye promise to help me? Did ye wish to call him down now?"

"Aye. If ye dinnae mind, I'll arrange ye, and I promise to stand by ye when he lands. He'll be kind to ye." He grinned, his smile full of warmth and good cheer.

The man was near perfection.

"All right. Whenever ye wish." She acquiesced, just because she liked the idea of him being closer to her.

"May I touch ye?"

She nodded, thinking she'd like nothing more. She kept that thought to herself.

He reached for her hips and set her the way he wished, then came around and stood behind her, lifting her arm up in front of her. He whistled once for Blue and he came back into view.

"Now just hold yer arm right there. Not in line with yer face but in front of the line of yer body."

Willum stepped closer until their bodies were flush. It was early spring and the wind blew a wee bit, but she'd never been warmer in her life. A heat consumed her, passing from his body to hers, and she was entranced, waiting to see if he said anything. But he didn't, instead moving so his chin was nearly atop her head. He whistled a second time, held her arm up strong and said, "Now keep yer arm right there."

Then he stepped back and came around to stand in front of her. She glanced at him and the expression on his face was so full of joy and appreciation of his falcon that she was humbled. If he would only look at her like that.

He lifted her elbow up just a touch. "Here he comes."

"What do I do?" Her voice came out in an odd titter, since she was a wee bit afraid.

"Naught. He'll come right to ye, I promise." Willum lifted his head and whistled again, and Blue came directly at her, its gaze now locked on her instead of on its master.

Such an exhilaration she'd never experienced before. The closer the bird came, the more her body reacted. She wished to look at Willum but didn't dare.

Willum whispered, "Good job. Keep yer eye on him. He'll land in a second, so just keep yer arm tight."

Not able to move, she squealed a wee bit with her mouth closed, her body humming with excitement as Blue landed directly on her arm, his eyes locked on hers before turning to Willum.

"Good job, Blue!" Willum gave him a treat, and the bird glanced back and forth between the two of them, probably looking for another treat.

"What does he eat? I thought they fed on smaller birds, but what do ye give him?"

"Depends on the time of the year. Mostly Blue prefers other birds, but he'll eat mice and rodents in the winter. I've even seen some of Da's birds go after rabbits, but we try to stop that because I love rabbits. Blue doesn't eat rabbit."

Her heart melted at the thought of this tall Highlander keeping pet rabbits. She had to see them someday. "What did ye give him?"

"Here. I have bits of dried meat. We make it just for the birds, for training. We feed whole prey for their meals."

She gave it a piece of meat and squealed when Blue took it from her.

"Is yer arm tired yet?"

"Aye, a wee bit."

"I'll show ye how to send him off."

He demonstrated with his arm what to do, then she copied his movement and Blue lifted off, his wings spreading with such grace and beauty, it humbled her.

"Many thanks for sharing Blue with me."

Willum smiled and reached for her hand. "Come. They are probably waiting for us. Time for a new patrol."

She clasped his hand and smiled. This patrol was looking better and better every minute.

CHAPTER THREE

THE GROUP MET by the stables, readying the horses, but Willum was surprised to see it was just Maitland and Dyna speaking with his father and Thea's sire, Donnan.

Maitland turned to include Willum and Thea in the conversation when he noticed their approach. "We will make a short trip and plan to return in a fortnight. We'll need reinforcements once winter begins to wane for good. As ye know, no' many try to venture far into the Highlands in this weather."

Snow fell in slow showers, a typical day in early spring. Willum enjoyed the snow because it covered the dead grass and made the landscape clean and bright. Except for the evergreen trees and shrubs, the bare branches of most trees made for a dull view.

But snow made the view of the forested hills spectacular.

Wulf came out in a hurry, all flushed. "We canno' join ye. My apologies, but Reyna is no' well."

Dyna spun around and asked, "What is the problem?"

Surprised by Dyna's question, Thea glanced at Willum before looking back to her sire, who shrugged.

Wulf said, "She just heaved everything up all over the hall. Dinnae go in—'tis no sight she wants to share. And she's upset because Gwyneth and Brenna arenae here. We canno' go along, but who is the closest healer? Jennet and Brigid are gone. No Jennie. I'm at a loss. Any advice?"

Donnan said, "I'll fetch Bethia since she worked with her mother many times. She knows much about healing, at least enough to guess the problem. If I dinnae return before the rest of ye leave for yer patrol, Godspeed with ye all and see ye in a fortnight." He nodded to Maitland as if to remind him of the promise to return soon, then tossed a wink toward Thea.

"We may be back sooner if we dinnae have Wulf and Reyna with us," Maitland said. "I would no' engage unless we number at least six. This would be just a scouting mission. Ye accept that?" He glanced to Dyna, Willum, and Thea.

Thea nodded, and Willum could tell she was most anxious to leave. Then he looked to his sire to make sure he would not argue the circumstances.

Will said, "Nay, I think the four of ye can patrol. See what is out there. 'Tis cold enough to make it a short trip. Even though I see signs of springs, I doubt ye'll see much yet, not for another fortnight or two. In about a moon, activity will definitely pick up. The English dinnae take to cold verra well, especially anywhere near the Highlands."

Wulf, still unsettled said, "Dyna, have ye any idea what could be bothering my wife?"

Thea smiled, then hid it with a quick hand over her mouth. "Have ye considered she might be carrying? Some women get verra sick when a babe is on the way."

"Heaving?" Wulf's eyes widened. "Truly? Carrying a bairn inside could make her heave?"

Thea nodded. Willum was quite certain that thought had not occurred to the man. Even he'd heard comments about women who felt miserable while carrying.

Dyna didn't bother to hide her smile. "Many women do heave in the first few months. It usually passes, but it can be miserable for them. Especially in the early hours of the day."

Wulf arched a brow. "Carrying? Truly?"

Willum suspected that the poor man had no idea he'd repeated himself. The thought of his wife carrying had sent him into a dither. Wulf didn't wait for Bethia's return, choosing instead to spin on his heel and race back into the hall.

"I'll go after him," Willum's father said. "I remember the feeling well. Godspeed to ye all and safe travels."

Once his sire left, he said to Thea, "Hard to believe that the man who intimidated so many English soldiers can be brought to his knees by his wee wife." Willum couldn't believe how much Wulf had changed since marrying Reyna and finding more of his family. Perrin had turned out to be quite a blessing.

Dyna let out a very unladylike snort. "Happens to many of them."

Thea whispered, "He's so cute when he worries about Reyna."

Willum and the rest mounted their horses. He had an odd feeling in his belly, wanting to leave as fast as they could. He had a sudden urge to get away, much as he'd felt in the hall earlier that day.

After living his life in the outdoors—sleeping, hunting, fishing—he had no interest in living inside. He had agreed to travel to Ramsay land with his parents, but every time they made the journey, he cringed when he had to spend a great amount of time in the castle. He'd been forced to adjust to living in a small cottage in the winter with just his small family, but large castles were just overflowing with people. Too many for his comfort.

Someone in Edinburgh once called him claustrophobic, a new word he added to his vocabulary because it seemed accurate. He could only stay inside four walls and a roof for a short time, especially a space as large as the hall of a castle. It was more the number of people he would be forced to be around, not as much the size of the building.

In his mind, his time was best spent with his birds, his rabbits, and Wenna's dogs. And a new companion he now favored above the animals.

Thea Douglas.

"Let's be off," Dyna said, motioning for them to leave. Thea questioned which way they were headed. South was the only word Willum heard, but that was all he needed to hear. It would make no sense to chase the English into the Highlands in the cold.

Thea and Dyna rode side by side, and he came behind, making it difficult for him to speak with her. No matter. He took the time to admire the swell of her fine arse in her leggings, reminding himself how perfect it had felt to have her soft curves pressed against his body when he'd been teaching her about Blue. He'd had to step away before his member betrayed him, standing in salute to the perfect form it was nestled against.

The lass was beautiful, skilled, intelligent, soft. All those things he already knew, and now he knew how easy she was to talk with and how wonderful she felt nestled against him.

He needed to be out in the wilderness with Thea Douglas, free to roam and enjoy each other. If they were fortunate, their patrol would be uneventful, and he'd have the opportunity to learn more about her.

If Thea was the type of lass who wished to live her life indoors, they would never suit. He hoped it was not so, but was unsure how to ask her such a question. The fact that she lived in a small cottage away from the castle gave him hope. That much he could handle, as long as it wasn't filled with a score of people or more.

Once they made it off Ramsay land and headed south on the main path, they arranged themselves in groups of two, Maitland and Dyna ahead of him and Thea.

Perfect. Now he had to come up with something to chat about. Fortunately, Thea managed it for him.

"So what do ye feel is yer purpose in life, Willum? My sire is always asking me that question or similar things. What would I like to do with my life? What would I like to be? A healer for people? A healer for animals like my mother? An archer? A spy? Or a mother of many bairns?"

"And do ye answer him?"

She shook her head emphatically, biting her lip. "Nay. I have no idea. Well, I must admit, there seems to be something always niggling at the back of my mind, something that wishes to push me in one direction or the other. But I can never put my finger on exactly what it is. I hope to find the answer to that question out on patrol. Away from the usual day-to-day responsibilities and activities. I think being away opens up my mind to other possibilities. How about ye?"

"I dinnae know. I love training falcons and I love to hunt. I like archery, but I think I prefer my sword. Mama often asks me if I wish to be a Ramsay or Grant guard." He shrugged. "I've thought of them all, but nothing wins my favor over another. I'm uncertain."

"What about patrol?"

"This I prefer over being a guard, but mostly because it allows me to be outdoors. I've spent most of my life sleeping in a cave or under the stars, so living in a large keep with so many people about is difficult for me. I probably sound foolish." He glanced over at Thea's profile, her loose hairs flying back from her face. "We did spend many winters in a small cottage, but that never bothered me, though I still snuck outside whenever I could. But the great halls in many castles filled with people, guards sleeping on the floors in winter to keep warm, dogs looking for food scraps. Too much for me. I'm pleased that Ramsay Castle is never that busy. Building accommodations for the guards near the stables is a wise idea that many should consider for their men." He could smell a brief scent of something sweet and stared at her again. Her skin was as clear as the petal of the finest flower, and he bet it had the same aroma.

Or perhaps sweeter.

Her lips were a rosy red in the cold, softly plump in her lower lip. Would he ever dare to taste her? How he hoped he would have the opportunity.

"Nay, I understand. Tell me more about the cottage ye spent time in. My parents dinnae like the keep either. My father prefers the quiet, and my mother prefers to listen to the birds in the morn, but we stay inside where it is warm. I love a large hearth when the snow falls. Ye dinnae ever wish for warmth in the winter?"

"My mother insisted on it many winters. Mostly when we were young and when she had the wee bairn…"

Thea's expression changed instantly into sadness, the same reaction everyone had when his mother's loss of her bairn was mentioned.

His whole family's loss. He'd have loved to have another sister.

"I forgot about that," she said, looking up at the sky for a moment. "How old was the lass?"

"She was less than a year, but she was tiny when she was born. Mama took her to Cameron land and then Ramsay land to try to help her to gain more weight, but nothing worked. Papa found us a cottage when Mama was carrying and we stayed there when it was coldest, but even that could no' warm up wee Annis. It was a difficult time."

Difficult was hardly the word he would use if he were to truly discuss his mother's descent into sorrow. The day they'd lost Annis, his father had brought his mother to her parents on Ramsay land and taken Willum and Wenna to stay with the Cameron clan. He and Wenna had stayed there for many weeks before they'd seen their parents again. Jennie Cameron had been a godsend to both of them, fussing over the two of them as if they were her own.

The depth of pain in his mother's eyes had left an indelible mark on his soul. But they'd carried on. A puppy, the smallest in Torrian's litter that year, joined their family. This dog became Wenna's, but the puppy had brought joy and smiles back into their lives. Wenna had named the puppy Sunny, and she still followed Wenna wherever she went, even on occasional patrols.

His memories were interrupted by a hand that held fast to his upper arm, stopping him in his tracks.

Thea pointed at something to their right. Maitland and Dyna had missed the rustling in the trees.

What the hell was making it?

CHAPTER FOUR

THEA'S HEART NEARLY broke in two. "Willum, look. A fawn caught in some kind of trap. We have to free it." She turned her horse in the direction of the young deer, making the quick decision that she would explain herself to Maitland and Dyna after she set the poor thing free.

"Thea, hold. We need to check with the other two."

Maitland and Dyna had ridden far enough ahead of Thea and Willum that they hadn't noticed they'd stopped.

"But I see the mother behind her." Then she gasped. She wondered if Willum had seen the same thing she just had—three men hiding in a copse of oak trees not far off. Apparently, the mother hadn't noticed or she would have taken off. Nor must they have noticed the doe, or they would have killed her already.

"And I see the hunters," Willum whispered. "I'll go with ye. We'll explain ourselves later."

Thea nodded and spurred her horse toward the poor deer. "Shield me while I set her free."

Willum nodded. "Go. I'll be nocked and ready to fire."

Thea reached for her dagger in her boot, making sure it was there before she jumped off her horse. She slapped her mare's haunch to move her a wee bit away. Thea knew she'd not leave, but she didn't want her in the line of any hunter's arrow.

She stepped toward the fawn. As she got closer, she could see that its hind leg was stuck in some odd contraption. The doe backed away nervously but didn't flee. Thea guessed that since she was moving quietly and slowly, the doe had decided to stay and see what happened.

"Willum, protect the mother too."

As soon as the hunters noticed her, one bellowed at her. "Leave it be. We caught it fair and square! You have no right to our quarry."

She knew by the accent they were English. Were they from Berwick Castle or the Borderlands? She had no idea and didn't care, but she had to do her best to free this innocent animal.

There was a rope around its leg and an odd metal ring attached to it. She cut the rope just as she heard someone shout her name.

"Thea, get yer arse out of there. Ye are about to be attacked!" Dyna's shout carried over the voices of the hunters, but she ignored it too. One look into the wee babe's frightened gaze told her she was staying. Those men were not going to make this creature nor its mother their next meal.

The poor animal reacted to all the shouting around it, shaking so hard in fear, Thea wanted to cry. The mother began to pace at all the chaos—the hunters in the trees and Willum, Dyna, and Maitland and their restless horses on the path. An arrow sliced through the air over the doe's head, and Thea said a quick prayer that she would not be hit.

"I'll set ye free, little one. Yer mother is waiting for ye."

As she worked to free the animal, she tried to keep a careful watch on the hunters, but she couldn't watch the fawn and them at the same time. She heard a rustle and turned. They were headed for her, small swords poised to strike. Willum took one down, hitting his leg with his arrow while Maitland bellowed and hefted his sword over his head with one arm.

That sent the other two men running in the other direction, but the one who'd been hit still acted half daft, cursing at her at the same time he pulled the arrow out of his leg. Blood gushed down the injured limb, soaking his trews as he hobbled after his companions.

Hellfire, but she was not moving until this beautiful animal was set free. She finally loosened the snare, but then noticed the open wound where the trap had chafed the fawn's leg raw. She pulled the salve out that she always carried tucked in her tunic and covered the wound as quickly as she could.

Dyna dropped down next to her. "Are ye out of yer mind? Ye're risking all our lives for this one fawn."

"I could no' leave it." Something inside her told

her it was her job to save this animal, and she was powerless to ignore that command. "I dinnae know why, but I was unable to stop myself."

Once the wound was covered, she picked up the fawn, managing to get to her feet with the deer in her arms. She hugged her close, looking about for her mother.

She spoke soothing words to the animal, as her mother had taught her long ago. *It matters no' what ye say since they dinnae understand ye, but the tone of yer voice can calm even the wildest of creatures.* The wee creature's tremors slowed in her arms.

She nearly stepped away from the tree that she'd sheltered behind, but Dyna stilled her. "Maitland and Willum are following the hunters. Make sure the English are long gone before ye move."

The stillness of the forest was slowly returning, and in response, the doe stepped closer to Thea, though it remained at a safe distance.

A moment later, three men bolted out of the far copse on horseback, heading south. One of them called out, "You'll pay for stealing our food!"

Thea was not concerned. Willum and Maitland soon rode out of the trees, their weapons held loose at their sides. They turned back toward the women, but stopped when they saw Thea carrying the fawn toward its mother. Once she was close enough, she knelt down and set the baby down to see if it would walk. The animal tested its leg and bleated to its mother, who answered quickly, as if encouraging it to move on its own. A few moments later, the youngster tentatively took four steps then shot toward its waiting mother. Mama nuzzled it, then they both took off into the woods, disappearing in an instant.

Thea smiled when Dyna patted her shoulder. "Well done, lass." She didn't even try to stop the few tears that escaped and rolled down her cheeks.

"I had to. I'm sorry, but…"

"I agreed to help," Willum said. "It was not just Thea's fault."

His support squeezed her heart a wee bit.

"Dinnae do it again, either of ye. Ye risked all of our lives." Maitland sheathed his sword and gestured back toward the path.

"But it needed our help. I had to do something." She didn't follow Maitland's reasoning. "Could ye have ignored it?"

"Ye took a serious risk, Thea. Was the fawn's life worth yer own or Willum's, if that arrow had hit either of ye instead of flying blindly over yer head? Did ye know the hunters were there when ye made yer move, or how many there were?"

"Nay, but it would no' have changed my mind. And I convinced Willum to help me." Thea glanced at Dyna, looking for her support.

Dyna's words surprised her. "I would have looked around for the person or persons who had set that trap before going after it. Ye were careless, lass. Fortunately, all ended well."

Thea had no words. No defense of her actions came quickly to mind, and she was unable to think of anything that could explain how she'd been compelled to act. Perhaps she could have made a better assessment of the situation before acting.

"Next time, ye confer with one of us first, lass. If no', this will be yer last patrol," Maitland said.

Thea swallowed hard at the declaration, but she couldn't argue. She also couldn't change what was in her heart.

And she didn't really understand it herself. She'd done something irrational. Her parents had taught her better. Her father had shown her how to analyze something carefully before acting—it was how he created his tools and inventions; and her mother had always shown her how to care for animals safely, first and foremost.

"Forgive me," she finally admitted. "That was indeed careless of me. My father would have chastised me also."

"And now, three men plan to avenge this deed. I pray they canno' keep up with us," Maitland said. "But ye are young. Ye will learn, lass. Ye did a fine job rescuing the animal. It had a better outcome than it would have if ye had ignored it."

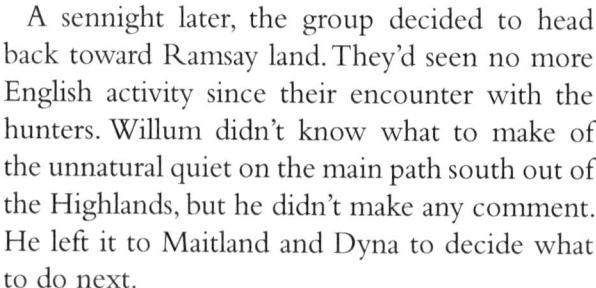

A sennight later, the group decided to head back toward Ramsay land. They'd seen no more English activity since their encounter with the hunters. Willum didn't know what to make of the unnatural quiet on the main path south out of the Highlands, but he didn't make any comment. He left it to Maitland and Dyna to decide what to do next.

Willum moved his horse closer to Thea. He

could tell she was still upset about the encounter with the fawn and its mother, though it had been a long time since they'd discussed it. He thought her unnaturally quiet.

"Are ye well, Thea?"

She glanced over at him and gave him a quick smile. "I'm fine. I'm just upset with myself for how I acted. The thought of the arrow hitting ye was a shock. I should not have been so careless. I dinnae know how to explain it, but I'm driven by unknown forces sometimes. Do ye ever feel that way?"

Truthfully, he did not, but he wished to answer her in a way that wouldn't upset her. "I think being on patrol can make anyone behave in odd ways. 'Tis hard to be on alert at all times. From what I've learned from our many cousins, patrol can go in many directions." That was an honest statement, and this was certainly a relatively quiet patrol. Unlike the few that preceded this one.

"So true. I would no' like to encounter anything like Isla and Grif endured, or even one similar to what confronted Ysenda and Lewis in the avalanche."

She stared straight ahead, and he wished she would share all her thoughts with him. Something seemed to be bothering her, but he had no idea what it could be.

"At least we have no' seen the bastards again, wherever they were from," he said.

"They were English. I'm sure of it. Their accents gave them away."

Willum chuckled. "And their paltry weapons.

That arrow couldn't have done any damage if ye'd been a horse length in front of the fool."

Thea snorted, then looked as embarrassed as he'd ever seen her. He laughed even louder at her reaction.

"I heard that, Thea Douglas," Dyna said, as she whirled her head around to laugh at her. "I could hear it up here."

"Well, they were English. Those swords were hardly a threat against Maitland's weapon."

"I agree with that assessment. Why they were this far north, I dinnae know. But it has been long enough that I dinnae believe they are following us," Dyna answered.

Their current patrol group of four continued north in peace until dusk neared. Maitland indicated a clearing and cave they could spend the night in, one Willum knew well. As they neared the cave, a loud rustling and snorting reached them.

Maitland's hand rose, and they all stilled.

He directed Dyna to move to the opposite side of the path and for Thea and Willum to stay back and ready their bows.

The rustling came from the bushes ahead, growing louder every moment, until a wild boar burst onto the path and headed straight for their horses.

"Shoot it!" Maitland yelled.

Willum reacted instantly, setting his mount after the boar while Dyna went in the opposite direction.

"Thea, stay back," Maitland yelled. "There are

two others coming from the left." He pointed just as the other animals burst out of the trees straight for Thea. Maitland was a swordsman, not an archer, so he was little help in this trouble.

Willum's arrow hit the first beast in the flank at the same time Dyna's hit him on the other side, dropping it to the ground as it squealed in pain. The noise set the other two boars reeling in the opposite direction, one for Maitland and one for Thea.

"Dyna, take Maitland's. I'll go for the other," Willum shouted, but Dyna had already taken aim and fired, striking the one in its back end. A direct hit, but not enough to stop it. It ran a ragged path, squealing and snorting in a fury. Thea rose in her stirrups, urging her horse steadily along, and fired, hitting the boar at an angle behind its front leg. The boar gasped, staggered, and toppled, its lungs clearly punctured.

Willum would have loved to stare at Thea's skill, but he couldn't, instead turning to deal with the final beast. But he watched with shock as Thea came up and aimed straight at the boar, striking it down with one arrow.

Most animals took two or three arrows to take them down. Not when Thea Douglas was the hunter.

He'd never admit to anyone how appealing that made her to him. How could he explain to anyone that observing her body heaving with exertion, her face now wild with a smile, gave him one of the hardest erections he'd had in a long time?

In that instant, Thea became the most exotic beauty he'd ever seen.

He knew his purpose now—to court Thea and make her his.

If he only knew how to go about it.

CHAPTER FIVE

THEY ATE WELL that night, with plenty of roast pork, which Thea liked better than other meats. Venison came from such beautiful animals that she couldn't partake, and she even had trouble eating rabbit stew, though hunger forced her to eat when she didn't always admire the choices.

Boars were only good for eating, in her eyes. The group sat around the fire and feasted, laughing mostly about how Thea learned to balance on a horse so well.

"Grandda taught me. I tried to stand on my saddle the way Aunt Lily could, but I dinnae have the balance she had. She's so thin, and I think that gives her an advantage. But Grandda said to try settling my knees just so, which gave me enough height so I could aim better. And my dear horse is so responsive. I named her Blossom after Aunt Lily, but she is my favorite mare, and she is lovely to ride."

Maitland gave a nod of affirmation. "Uncle Quade was amazing to watch on his horse. I've heard that story retold many times."

"Which one?" Dyna asked. "The love story with Aunt Brenna?"

Maitland nodded, his mouth full of meat.

"Other than my parents' love story, Grandda's and Grandmama's is my favorite," Thea said. "I dinnae know how Grandmama dinnae die of sheer fright coming so close to the cliff she almost went over."

Willum picked up the tale with a smile. "And I can picture Uncle Quade and my grandda yelling at him. I can hear Grandda as if I were there behind him."

Dyna let out a heartfelt sigh. "I love the old sibling stories. Quade and Logan running around as wee laddies must have been a sight to see."

Thea caught the faraway look in her gaze, and stayed silent, not wanting to disturb the other woman.

Dyna whispered, "I miss *Seanair* so much."

Seanair was the Gaelic term for grandfather. Alexander Grant had passed on last year, and his clan had certainly had a difficult time accepting it. He was fondly remembered by all in the Highlands.

"We all miss Alex, but he left us with many tales to share. I'd love to talk more, but I'm exhausted." Maitland threw the bones off into the woods for the animals. "I'm ready to sleep. On the morrow, we'll head home. I dinnae see why we canno' leave a few days early so we can take advantage of the cold temperature and bring a boar home to our families. They'll appreciate it. The temperature is perfect to keep the meat from spoiling."

"As long as no animals smell them this eve, we'll be fine," Dyna said, getting to her feet. "But there are enough bones and meat left out here to confuse any scavengers. We should leave at first light."

"Agreed," Maitland said.

Dyna looked at Thea and Willum. "Maitland and I are both going to Menzie land. Thea, I know where ye are headed, but Willum? Where are ye going? Will yer parents still be on Ramsay land?"

"I'm no' sure. I'll escort Thea home, then check to see if they are there. But ye need no' worry about me as ye know how I am. Sometimes, I prefer to be like Grandda and wander from one place to another. If they arenae there, I'll go to our cottage."

Maitland turned to Willum before standing up to stretch. "I'm only planning a sennight's rest before going back south. I expect a messenger from King Robert in a few days. I'll have our instructions then. He'll be pleased to hear that we found no English soldiers on this short patrol. Those English reivers dinnae count. Even that is good news."

Dyna nodded, flinging her pale white plait over her shoulder with a hard flick of her wrist. "Aye, they need to keep their arses south of the Borderlands where they belong. Reivers included."

The group cleaned up the clearing and headed into the cave after settling the horses. Dyna and

Thea went toward the back of the cave, where it would be a wee bit warmer.

Willum came in and tossed a small roll to each of them. "I nearly forgot to give these to ye both. A gift for ye from Mama."

"What are they?" Thea asked, looking at the fine brown fur on one side of the roll.

"Open it and see," he instructed, his hands lazily on his hips. "I think ye'll like them."

Dyna fussed over hers. "Is this one of those long pieces yer mama makes from deerskin? This one is so large that she's sewn pelts together. Are they no' meant to protect ye from the cold?"

He nodded. "And the rain. Water will not seep through them, even from the soggiest ground. She uses two layers and puts something between them, though I know no' what it is. They arenae thick enough to cushion ye, but they promise to keep ye dry and warm."

Thea opened hers and spread it out on a nearby boulder. "Oh, my. This took Maggie a long time, did it no'?" She ran her hand down the soft fur, admiring the careful stitches between the different pelts. "Some of mine are rabbit."

"Aye, she works on many over the winter. Her work got her through some difficult times, but they are a treat to have with ye. Wenna has several."

"Many thanks to ye. It will be very welcome between me and the cold stone of the cave."

"Sweet dreams to both of ye," Willum said.

Thea fell asleep thinking of turquoise eyes, her hands rubbing the fine fur of her gift.

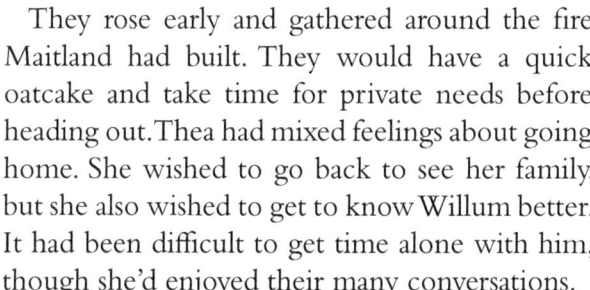

They rose early and gathered around the fire Maitland had built. They would have a quick oatcake and take time for private needs before heading out. Thea had mixed feelings about going home. She wished to go back to see her family, but she also wished to get to know Willum better. It had been difficult to get time alone with him, though she'd enjoyed their many conversations.

"How many do ye think will be along for the next patrol?" Thea asked, moving a log closer to the fire and rubbing her hands together.

Willum sauntered out from behind a group of trees looking as if he was ready for the king's court. Why did men look even better all tousled and sleepy? She was quite certain that her looks were not nearly as pleasing as Willum's this early in the morn.

"I hope Reyna and Wulf will join us," Dyna said, "but if she is truly carrying, they may not. Ysenda willnae be ready yet. Probably Wenna and Tevis. He promised to return within a sennight so I'm hoping he will be there, ready and waiting. I'm going into the bushes. Dinnae put the fire out until I warm myself one more time, Maitland."

"I vow to keep it going just for ye, Corbett." He grinned and handed a hunk of roasted pork and an apple to Thea. He sat down on a boulder across from Thea and ate his own piece of fragrant meat.

"Think ye Isla and Grif will come along with

Tevis?" She hoped for a larger group next time. Having more in their group made her feel safer. But was it truly safer? A larger group was certainly harder to hide.

"Nay. I think Grif will come next patrol, but it strikes me that Isla wants naught to do with winter weather. She loves to battle in spring, so she'll return eventually, but no' yet."

"And the others?"

Maitland shrugged. "There have certainly been many weddings and betrothals, which pleases me, especially since I am fortunate to be one of them. But I think we'll be limited in number until summer comes. Once summer is here, I expect to see Ceit and Brin and Ysenda and Lewis. Steinn could return with Tevis. Reyna and Wulf could be out for a year if she is carrying. And I'm hoping that now that Ysenda is out, mayhap Gavin and Merewen will allow Elisant along. We shall see."

"Eli wishes to come?" She loved her cousin Eli. She was sassy, funny, and smart and always brightened whatever group she was with.

"She does, but Merewen didnae wish both daughters together. Errol stays with his sire, so he'll no' be along. Now that Ysenda is no' patrolling, we'll see if Eli joins us. We could use her. I havenae seen her shoot, but..." He shrugged. "Any granddaughter of Aunt Gwyneth's is welcome."

"And Cadyn?"

Maitland snorted. "I dinnae think ye'll ever see Cadyn on patrol again unless his grandfather patrols. I was glad he came when he did, glad he met Tryana, but they are happy at home. And they are quite certain she is carrying too. After weddings come bairns."

"Ye included."

"And I canno' tell ye how pleased I am about that."

"We are all happy for ye, Maitland. He'll be a fine laddie," she said. Maitland and Maeve were so convinced they were having a boy that everyone else went along with them.

"So ye will stay on patrol?"

Willum sat down and chewed on an apple, listening to the conversation.

"Aye, for now," Thea replied. "I know no' how long, but right now, I'd like to travel, I think."

"But yer parents dinnae wish ye to go far," he stated.

"They want me close, and I wish to leave to find my true place."

Willum chuckled. "And I wish to go back and check on my parents all the time. I worry about them alone in the woods. Ye wish to travel, and I wish to stay close to home."

"And Thea likes crowds while ye prefer to hide from crowds. What would ye choose to do with yer life, Willum?" Maitland asked.

"Like Da, I guess. Find a woman to love and have bairns. Live in the wild, but I also love to travel. I guess I'm no' sure what I wish to do. They ask me about being a guard, but I dinnae know if that appeals to me. Mayhap a spy for my country."

"And ye, Thea?"

She shrugged. "I dinnae know."

"A healer of animals like yer mama? 'Tis a rare skill."

She shrugged again.

"A healer like yer grandmama?"

Another shrug. Nothing felt quite right yet.

"I hope ye find yer answer," Willum said, tossing the boar bones over his shoulder. "If not on patrol, then at least when the need for our patrols ends."

"True, but will it ever be finished? Will the English ever go home and leave the Scots to live our lives?" Thea wished to shout this sentiment from the top of a mountain.

"Nay," Dyna called out from where she tended her horse. "They plan to torture us for eternity, I swear."

Thea mulled over this answer, but she couldn't argue with her. Her father often said that men loved to battle, fight, and stir up feuds. He said the Scots would fight with the English forever. Their conflict would only stop temporarily, and it would be because of another group for the English to battle—the Welsh or the Irish. If then. Even fighting the French hadn't seemed to distract the English king from his desire to conquer the Scots.

Dyna Grant wasn't paying close attention to her surroundings, and Thea saw movement in the bushes not far from her. Thea stood up and nearly shouted, but the hard glare Dyna cast her way stopped her.

Dyna had already seen him, apparently. The sly figure crept up behind her, ignoring the fact that there were three others nearby. The man must be the worst fool.

He leapt out of the bushes and tried to drag Dyna away, a wide grin on his face, mumbling to Dyna as if his words justified his actions. "It has been too long since I had a lively female. I promise not to take too much of yer time, lass."

Dyna swung around, her dagger piercing his leg, and he let out a howl and loosened his grip. The moment Dyna could jerk free, she kicked him in his bollocks and his head fell forward with a painful grimace. Dyna brought her knee up under his chin, and his head snapped back.

He fell to the ground in a heap, cradling his private area and his leg, moaning in pain.

Maitland had a wide grin on his face when he called out, "Need any help, Dyna?"

"I have everything under control, Menzie. Daft bastards keep me on my toes." Dyna strode over and yanked her dagger out of her attacker's thigh, cleaning it on the man's tunic. "Touch me again, ye bastard, and I'll cut off yer bollocks."

The man forced himself to his feet and staggered off, fear written across his face.

Those few moments brought a sudden revelation, and Thea Douglas knew she would never be the same again. She knew what her new goal would be for her life.

"I need to be just like Dyna."

Willum turned his head to her. "Why?"

She shrugged. "My sire tells me I need to have a goal, a purpose. I always tell him I have none. But now I do. I wish to be just like Dyna, able to fight off any attacker on my own. Kill the men who attack the good animals. I might like to defend lasses who are attacked. Make their attackers pay for their transgressions just like Dyna did. He'll no' be able to swiv any lass for a while."

Willum arched his brow. "Ye are no' far from one purpose I dinnae talk much about."

"What is yers?"

"To save any girl who is being attacked."

She nodded, thinking on his parents. His mother, Maggie Ramsay, was one of the adopted daughters of Gwyneth and Logan Ramsay, her aunt and uncle. She'd been adopted when Gwyneth had found her chained to a tree outside a fine home, a punishment for dropping a platter. "Yer mother. I recall."

"Aye. Most everyone knows about the platter, but no' many know that Randall Baines abused her. So I fight for lasses who canno' fight for themselves. And ye can, Thea Douglas. I dinnae believe a single man could successfully attack ye. What ye did with the boar proves that ye are a strong archer and equally good with a dagger. He'd regret his attack just as Dyna's attacker is right now."

"I hope I never find out," she mumbled as Dyna joined them.

"Mount up. We should move on in case the bastard has any friends." Dyna spit over her shoulder, a bit unladylike, but an appropriate send-off for the bastard who dared to touch her.

"Dyna," Maitland asked after he mounted. "Was

the fool English or a Scot? Could it have been one of the men we met earlier hunting the deer?"

"A Scot. We need no' search for his friends. We can carry on as planned." But then she paused, as if another thought occurred to her. She turned her horse to face Maitland. "Why do ye ask, Menzie? I dinnae like the way this conversation is headed."

Dyna did indeed have an eerie sense of what was happening, long before others did. Certainly Thea, because she had no idea what the woman was referring to. But it soon became clear how accurate Dyna's small premonitions were.

"Because I just discovered we have a problem. I dinnae know why I didnae check earlier," Maitland said, studying the wrapped meat they'd butchered. "Some of the boar meat is missing."

They'd butchered the boar and left the carcasses in an area a good distance back to keep the animals away. Maitland had wrapped the meat carefully in the leather wrappings they used to transport meat safely, hoping to keep the aroma from drawing other animals.

"How much is missing?" Dyna asked, dismounting to look over his shoulder at the package. "I hope no' much. We need that meat."

"Nay, but one large slab is missing. And it wasn't taken by an animal. Someone undid the bindings and removed the meat, then retied it. I wouldn't have noticed it if I hadn't squeezed the bag."

"Mayhap the Scot who tried to attack Dyna took it," Willum suggested.

Maitland looked back over his shoulder and

scanned the entire camp. "Probably. I'll accept that and not search for it. I've the feeling we need to take our leave now."

Dyna said, "I agree. I have an odd feeling creeping up the back of my neck."

"What kind?" Thea asked, knowing Dyna had powerful seer skills.

She whispered, "The English kind."

"Aye, I feel the same," Maitland said. "But I wish to be certain we dinnae lead any visitors back to Menzie or Ramsay land. We'll take a wide path north since we have plenty of time. If we see no one, then we can go to Menzie land for a quick visit, then head to Ramsay land and gather our forces for a larger patrol."

"Ye just wish to see Maeve again. Ye dinnae fool me." Dyna patted his shoulder and mounted her horse again.

Maitland grinned. "That I do. I like to keep my wife happy. And ye can visit with yer husband and bairns since he's on Menzie land at present. Willum and Thea, will ye stop with us or go on to Ramsay land? Ye know it is no' much farther."

"I'll go on to Ramsay land, if Willum is willing," Thea said. She wished to get home and share her revelation with her papa and mama. Excitement still thrummed through her. She was choosing to ignore the mistake she made earlier in their trip, including the odd feelings she'd been having.

Willum pulled abreast of Thea. "I'm pleased to go along with ye, Thea. I need to see where my parents are."

"Thank ye, Willum. I promised my parents I'd

be home every fortnight, so they'll be happy to see me home early. And if yer parents have gone, ye know ye are always welcome on Ramsay land. Mayhap the group will be back from Black Isle. I have no' seen Grandmama in a while. I like to make sure she is hale."

"Aunt Brenna will live forever."

She threw him a stern glance. "Dinnae jest. I'll be destroyed when she passes."

"We all will."

She had a sudden odd feeling course through her insides along with a quick vision. As if death were nearby.

"What is it?" Dyna asked. "Are ye hale?"

"I'm fine, I just had this odd feeling."

Dyna, who had a reputation as a seer, arched a brow at Thea. "Can ye describe it?"

Thea sighed. "I just dinnae want any more deaths. 'Tis what the odd feeling was telling me. 'Tis someone else's time." She shivered and not from the cold.

"Do ye often have these premonitions?"

"Nay, Dyna. I leave those to ye. I dinnae want them."

Dyna sighed. "Unfortunately, ye canno' will them away. Accept them and learn. The next question is who? Could ye see anyone?"

"Nay," she lied.

There was no point in telling Dyna the truth: she had seen a man, and she had no idea who it was, but one thing she knew for certain.

He was following her.

CHAPTER SIX

WILLUM FOLLOWED THEA onto Ramsay land, letting his breath out because they'd made it safely. He didn't like traveling alone, and two was not much better than one, especially after the odd occurrences at the cave. But he'd never admit to Thea how unsettled he'd been about the end of their journey. After all that had transpired, Maitland and Dyna had escorted them all the way to Ramsay land before turning back to their destination, something he'd appreciated. The group had talked little, instead focused on observing their surroundings.

They still had no idea who had stolen the meat. But they'd made it back safely. He hoped the odd occurrences did not bring his nightmares back. He'd had them for many years after he'd become lost that one time.

He loved living outdoors, but not alone. One bad childhood experience had left an indelible mark on his mind. He hoped there would be a few more on their next journey that was to take place in a sennight. His preference was a crowd of ten, at least, when on the road. Then he felt safer.

"I heard that, Willum." Thea glanced over her shoulder at him.

"What? I didnae say anything." Confused, he was afraid to ask exactly what was going on in her mind. He wished to impress Thea, not show any of his weaknesses.

"Ye didnae have to. I could hear yer sigh of relief from here. Ye dinnae like traveling with me?"

"Nay, no' true. I love traveling with ye. But I prefer to have a few more with us. I'm used to patrols having larger numbers. And I had one time in my past when I was alone in the woods, and I dinnae like to remember it."

"What happened?"

He hated talking about it, but he was curious to hear Thea's thoughts on his experience. "I was young—just a wee lad. My family was traveling, and I got lost. I could no' locate my parents, and when ye are in the middle of a forest, it can be frightening." That was the most important part of the memory and enough to reveal for now. The rest he did his best to keep hidden, even though the tendrils came out to grab him occasionally. "But ye dinnae mind being alone, Thea?"

"I prefer a larger group when we are in battle, of course. Being alone frightens the hell out of me on patrol. But being alone in our woods does no' bother me."

"I'm the odd one," Willum admitted. "I dinnae like crowds because I lived in the wilderness, but I dinnae like to be alone either. Nearly opposite feelings, but they are different to me." He didn't know how to explain that turning around in a forest and not knowing which way to go was one of his worst experiences ever. "Being lost in the woods alone at the age of six truly scared me out of my wits." The older he got, the weaker the memory became, but it still bothered him, forcing him to push it out of his mind whenever it reared itself.

"Oh, I believe ye, Willum. And I must add that when I'm in the forest at home, I always have my dogs with me. So I'm never truly alone. They would go for help if necessary. How scary for ye." She waved to her great uncle, who was approaching quickly. "Uncle Logan!" she called out.

Glad to be saved by his grandfather, Willum shoved the tendrils out of his mind, focusing on the nice arse bouncing on the horse in front of him. Then he thought of the tales of Grandmama and turned his eyes away. Even though Thea was not a grandbairn to Logan and Gwyneth, they were still quite protective of her. He'd heard tales of how protective Logan had been with Thea's mother, Bethia. He'd saved her from a terrible fate, and Grandmama had pinned the villain to a tree by his bollocks.

That tale had been retold many times, and he'd taken it as the warning it was—no man threatened a Ramsay woman. He needed to act appropriately around Thea at all times to keep from being skewered.

"Thea, is that Willum with ye? Why are ye two alone? Ye should have more guards with ye." The man's gaze scanned the area looking for others.

She pulled her horse up as soon as Grandda stopped. "Dyna and Maitland just left us. They've stopped on Menzie land with plans to return here and gather the next patrol in a sennight. I'm glad to see ye are safely home. Who returned with ye?"

"Tevis and Alaric. Isla and Grif are no' returning yet. Too cold for Isla."

Willum was pleased to hear there were at least three more if Eli was going along. "Good additions for our next patrol. It willnae be just four of us. There could be at least seven."

"Aye, Eli is definitely going along," Grandda said. "Gavin has convinced Merewen she is strong enough to go along. Willum, yer parents left but Wenna has stayed. She'll be going along too. That would give ye eight."

Grandpapa turned his mount about, and the trio headed toward the castle.

Willum pulled his horse abreast of Thea. "Now we'll have a large group again. Eight suits me much better."

"Aye. I'm surprised but glad."

Grandda called out over his shoulder. "Dinnae be glad. They are all here because there is trouble in the Borderlands again, and King Robert wants ye there."

"What kind of trouble?"

"Ye'll no' know until ye get there. Whatever trouble the English can stir up, they will. Probably in Berwick or Ayr. Expect a challenging journey this time." Grandda snorted.

Willum glanced over at Thea, who grimaced. He could probably guess her thoughts were the same as his.

What the hell did Grandda mean by a challenging journey?

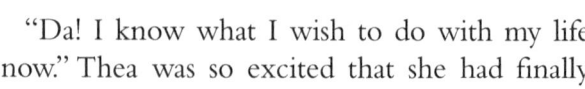

"Da! I know what I wish to do with my life now." Thea was so excited that she had finally found clarity in her thoughts that she had to share with her sire right away.

Willum had left her at her cottage and gone on to the keep to visit with Wenna. He'd told her he would probably seek out his parents before he returned, so she waved goodbye and off he went.

"Slow down, daughter," her father said, whistling for her mother. "Wait until yer mama comes. She'd like to hear this also."

She gave her father a big hug. "This was a wonderful journey."

"Ye fought off many?" He peered over Thea's shoulder to see if her mother was coming. He was busy working in his tool hut, perfecting pine boards.

"Nay, only a few. But there were Englishmen trying to hunt on our land, and they'd trapped a fawn. I couldnae let it happen. We also ran into three wild boar, but they didnae survive. And then later, Dyna fought off one reiver, but it was a Scot who dared to bother her." She grinned and pulled her hair out of its plait, swinging it wildly. "'Tis good to be home for a wee bit, Da. 'Twas cold out there, but Willum gave me one of his mother's fine skins to sleep on. Keeps ye warmer and drier."

"Bethia! Come on out." Her father raised his voice loud enough for her mother to hear. "Yer daughter is out here with me."

"I can find her, Da," she offered.

"Nay, no need." He nodded toward the cottage. Thea turned her head to see her mother approaching. Having greeted her in the house, she'd already greeted her and Lorana, who'd been sitting enjoying her porridge.

"I'm coming. What is it, Donnan?"

Her mother's puzzled look turned to her as soon as her sire pointed. "She has something to tell us."

"Wonderful. What news have ye?" Her mother folded her hands in front of her.

"I know what I wish to do with my life now."

"May I guess?"

"Go ahead," she replied, "but ye'll no' guess correctly." She tipped her head sideways, waiting for her mother's answer.

"Ye wish to marry Willum."

Her eyes widened, unable to contain her shock at that answer, which she hadn't expected. "Nay. Why would ye say such a thing?"

Her mother shrugged and glanced at her father who covered his mouth with his hand, hiding his smile for certain. "I dinnae know. It just popped into my mind. Mayhap a healer?"

"No' a healer."

"A healer for animals, like yer mother," her sire guessed, crossing his arms in front of him.

She shook her head.

Her mother guessed next. "Ye wish to be a creator like yer sire. Build things to make people's lives easier. A wonderful choice."

"Nay. Sorry, Papa." She leaned over and gave him a wee squeeze.

"I have no idea then," her mother said, tossing her hands up in the air.

"Dyna. I wish to be like Dyna."

Her parents glanced at each other, both puzzled. "What do ye mean? Lead patrols?" her father asked.

"Nay. Some reiver ran out of the woods and tried to drag her off, but she fought him off and made him run away. I wish to do the same. Go after any man who attacks women. Ye know it often happens, and I dinnae like it. I wish to teach them a lesson, like Dyna did."

Both parents stared at her, neither speaking.

"What? Is something wrong with Dyna?"

"Nay," her mother answered so quickly it startled her. "We love Dyna, but I believe her task in life is to protect Scotland and to care for her family. Look how she took care of Uncle Alex. She rarely left his side."

"Well, can I no' become the person who protects women from attackers? Why could I no' do that?"

Her mother looked at her father. "Yer turn. I'm needed back in the cottage. I have dinner cooking." She kissed Thea's cheek. "I'm glad ye are thinking on it. Ye will figure out what makes ye happy."

She didn't know how to answer that. This was more than being happy. If it were just that, she would ride her horse all day or play with her dogs or learn falconry or raise rabbits. In the summer, she'd swim in the loch every day if she could. It was about helping others. That was it. "But I'd like to help others, Da, no' just play to be happy. 'Tis what Lorana does and when ye grow up, ye must contribute to the clan. Do something purposeful. Make something like weapons or cook sweet treats or weave fine cloth. Look at all ye do, Da."

"I agree with everything ye've said, but…"

"But what? Why can I no' be like Dyna?" This had seemed such a simple solution, and she didn't understand why they hadn't been thrilled with her choice. Perhaps it had seemed too risky. That she could be attacked and unable to fight the men off?

"Have ye spoken with Dyna about this idea? Asked her how often she does what she did to that man? Ask her if she helps others on Grant land?"

She plopped down on a nearby boulder. "Nay, no' precisely, but I can on our next trip. Ye are hesitant. Why?"

"Ah, lass, 'tis a most noble cause, but most men hurt women in private. They like to inflict their punches where the bruises will no' be seen and knock them in the head so the bump is hidden. Catching someone in the act would be quite difficult. But I like the way ye are thinking. On yer next journey, talk with Dyna. She'll give ye some advice."

Disgruntled, she had the need for her dogs. "I'll think on it. Do ye need my help at all, Da?" She adored her father and loved working with wood.

"Nay, go relax. Visit with yer cousins. I hear ye are leaving again soon, though I do hope yer brother arrives before ye go. 'Twould be good for ye to visit for a wee bit."

"I know. I miss Drystan terribly."

"We all do, but 'tis no' the reason ye need to spend time with him. Ye know why."

She did, but she wasn't ready to discuss it with her sire. She preferred denial.

She scowled and took her leave before he brought up the exact subject she refused to discuss.

CHAPTER SEVEN

WENNA GREETED WILLUM with a sisterly hug when he reached Ramsay Castle. He helped himself to some food and a mug of ale before joining her at a table in the hall.

"Are our parents still here?" he asked.

"Nay. Ye just missed them. They left yesterday," Wenna said. "Da was talking about returning to their cottage. It's too cold for Ma this time of year."

"Then why didn't they stay here?" Willum asked. They were always welcome on Ramsay land.

Grandda joined them. "Yer mother knows yer sire prefers to live under the stars and that the only reason they even stay in a cave or cottage is for her, but her bones are getting older and she prefers the comfort of a soft heather mattress. Yer father prefers green moss. She's willing to compromise in the summer, but no' in the cold. She wishes to be warm and comfortable. But yer father was restless. So the compromise is the cottage, as ye know."

"Da had already been here for more than a fortnight," Wenna said. "Ye know how he gets."

"He was pacing, wasn't he?" Willum asked.

Grandda snorted. "By the time we returned, Will nearly hugged me and ran out the door as soon as I stepped inside. I knew they'd be leaving within two days. Though I suspect as he is getting on in years too, he may be happy to go to the cottage. These old bones of mine prefer a soft mattress to the hard ground of winter."

Wenna arched a brow. "Less than that—they left the next day. Da said he didn't care where they went as long as they left. He said they would return in a fortnight hoping to catch ye back from patrol, though who knows when they will return. But if they return, it will be a short visit. He does not intend to spend a long time here."

Willum knew that meant his parents were arguing about where to live. He knew where their first few stops after leaving Ramsay land usually were, so he would try those first. He had to agree with his grandsire that they had probably gone to their cottage, so that would be where he headed first. If he couldn't locate them within two days, then that meant they didn't wish to be found.

Willum finished his meal and rose. There was still enough light to set out today.

"I'll return in time for the next patrol. I wish to make a quick check on our parents. Make sure Mama is hale."

He hoped that on the next patrol, he could get closer to Thea. He couldn't think of a better reason to join patrol this time, but not until he saw his parents were both hale. He'd worried about his mother's health ever since she'd passed fifty winters several years ago. They were both getting on in years.

He just hoped he could find them. If he couldn't, usually Blue could locate his sire's falcons. As if on cue, Blue circled above his head as he guided his horse onto the path. A few moments later, the peregrine dove into the woods and came up with something in his beak. The bird was faster than any he'd ever seen.

Willum swung his route over near the Douglas cottage. He'd promised to let Thea know when he left. He wished he had a good reason to stop and visit, but he was pressed to continue his journey.

Thea was outside training her dogs. He pulled up far enough away that he wouldn't distract the dogs too much, but close enough for her to hear him.

"I'm going to visit my parents, and I will return in two days. I must hurry my trip because I dinnae know exactly where my parents are headed. Wenna said they were quite vague about their travels. I'm looking forward to being with ye on our next patrol."

"Godspeed and hurry back!" She blew him a kiss, which surprised him.

It also pleased him.

That kiss gave him motivation to speed his journey along, even if it only existed in the air.

It was nearly dusk when he located his parents in their cottage. He'd taken his time traveling, enjoying watching Blue in the clear sky above. Several falcons circled overhead, which gave him the clues he needed, and they were exactly where he expected them to be.

"Willum?" his father called out once he noticed his approach. "What brings ye along?"

"I wished to see how ye fare, Da. I was worried about the two of ye."

"We are fine. Ye need to stop remembering that one bad day. We'll no' be losing ye again."

Losing him. He supposed that was a good way to look at it.

"Have ye extra meat? I've not eaten since morn." He dismounted and pulled his saddlebags free.

"We have some smoked pork that Logan sent with us. There's plenty. Come inside, warm yerself. Yer mother will be pleased to see ye." His father brought out a bucket of oats for his horse.

"I'd love to join ye after I settle my mount. We killed three boars on our trip. Ate one and sent the rest to Menzie land." Willum omitted the rest of the story, that someone had stolen one of the slabs of meat. He settled his horse, brushing him down quickly and arranging the bucket of oats for him nearby, along with some fresh water from the rain barrel. Then he joined his parents at their hearth in the cottage. "Greetings to ye, Mama. Are ye no' glad to see the blue sky? The weather is improving. I look forward to spring."

"As do I," his mother mumbled, huddling under the blanket near the fire. He knew exactly what she meant. She wished to be wherever it was warm.

"It will be warm soon, Maggie," his father said, leaning down to kiss her cheek. "We're going to take a trip to Cameron land for a wee visit. We promised Sorcha we'd check on Ceit and Brin. And they allow us to sleep in Aedan's cottage, the one where the roof slides off so I can feel like I'm outside."

"Good. I'm glad," said Willum. His father had a stronger preference to the outdoors than he did, it seemed.

"So why have ye followed us? Please dinnae tell me 'tis still the old wound of yers." His sire gave him that odd look again. The one he hated.

"Da, can I no' just check on ye? Ye know I like to sleep under the stars too." Why did his father always question him when he checked on them?

"We're fine, son. Ye need no' check on yer mother. I take good care of her." He handed Willum a trencher with a cooked piece of pork he'd just warmed over the fire.

Sometimes Willum felt they did not want him around. Most parents never wanted their bairns to move out of their home or move away. His parents were happy when he left.

They never acted that way about Wenna.

His father sat down next to him, patted his knee and lowered his voice. "It only happened on one occasion. Ye need to stop fussing over it. It was such a small incident in yer life, a life of nearly three decades. Ye've been through so many other important events, I dinnae understand why it stays with ye so."

"Mayhap because ye keep reminding me of it, Da? Why must ye bring it up?" He did often think of it, but his father's constant mention of the incident did not help him one bit.

His father shrugged, embarrassment clear on his face. "Guilt, I guess. I still canno' believe we lost ye. I'll never forget it, Willum."

"Will, leave it be," his mother said. "I'm happy to see ye, Willum. I'd hoped ye would return before we left Ramsay Castle."

Willum had kept his thoughts to himself for so long that mayhap it was time to air his grievance. If they truly took the time to discuss what happened, perhaps it would not bother the two of them so often. He was going to share his thoughts. Just this once. "Da, it was not a small incident. Not to one of only six winters."

"But we found ye."

"Three days later! That was a verra long time to me."

"We are so sorry, Willum," his mother said. "I still dinnae know how it happened."

Willum didn't know either. He recalled how he'd gone to take care of his needs and a butterfly had happened along. Of course, he chased it, but apparently he had chased it for a much longer distance than he'd thought. By the time he'd finally lost the creature, he'd looked for his family only to discover that he didn't recognize the area he was in.

His father was gone and so was his mother.

He'd glanced overhead only to realize that dusk had descended and it was nearly impossible to see a bird in the sky, much less a falcon. His gut had wrenched enough that he'd nearly heaved up all he'd eaten, but he'd kept control, staying in place and calling for his parents.

Two more days and nights of calling for help, scrounging for food, and staring into the sky hoping for a sight of his father's birds. He had no idea where they were. Nightmares of reivers stealing him away, boars attacking him, or death from hunger haunted him. He had his bow and was skilled enough with it, but all he'd found to eat were berries.

He called out until his throat was raw. Sobbed until he had no more tears. The three days had felt like three years to him. Finally, he'd realized he needed to move. He had some idea which way they'd been going the day he'd wandered off, and he knew how to track the sun and the growth of moss on the trees to tell which direction was which. So he'd set out, his heart beating wildly with new fears that he'd just missed his father or gotten turned around.

When he'd finally found his way back to the cave, his mother had been there while his father was out looking for him.

"Mama!" He ran to her and threw himself into her warm arms, shivering from the cold of the autumn weather, unwilling to let her go for the longest time.

Finally she pushed him back, holding him at arm's length. "What happened, Willum? How did ye get lost? I feared we'd no' find ye until spring. Ye must never go so far from us again."

He'd swallowed hard, doing his best to curb his tears. "A butterfly. I wanted the butterfly."

When his father returned at nightfall, his horse was wet with sweat and Will hung his head with weariness.

"Papa!" Willum had called from the cave, and his father straightened.

"He's back? Ye are hale, Willum?"

"Aye, Papa. I chased a butterfly."

It had not been a small incident to him. In fact, some nights he still had the same nightmare of awakening in the middle of a forest alone, circling and looking for his falcon, his parents, his sister, anything at all that was familiar, but found nothing.

It had left such an impression on him that he swore he'd never be alone again. In fact, it was one of the reasons he had trained his own falcon. Blue was more than a pet, he was his friend.

An intense sense of exhaustion settled over him. "Do ye mind if I stay a night or two with ye? I'll return to Ramsay land in less than a sennight. I must ready myself for our next patrol."

"Willum?"

"Aye, Da?"

"Ye need to find someone. I hope ye do. Ye will make a fine father. I'm going for a wee stroll." His father clasped his shoulder and then strode out the door and into the woods.

Willum found his old bed in a separate chamber, covered with warm plaids and his mother's skins.

Even away from the hearth, he'd always been warm here. "I'll see ye on the morrow, Mama," he called out.

His mother stuck her head inside the door. "Happy dreams to ye, son. And I'm so sorry for yer terrible experience so many years ago. I wish I could erase it from yer mind."

"I'm fine, Mama. Dinnae worry yerself, but I am tired. I'll be here for a few days."

His mother nodded and moved back into the main room of the cottage, probably near the hearth, if he were to guess.

His father might not know it, but Willum's main goal in life was to find a partner, a wife, someone who would miss him if he left. Someone who would come looking for him right away. He wished to marry more than anything.

And he thought he might have finally found the woman he wanted by his side.

CHAPTER EIGHT

THREE DAYS AFTER her return from patrol, Thea's beloved brother Drystan arrived. He burst through the door, nearly breaking it from its hinges.

"Greetings all! And how does my dear sister fare?"

She bolted out of her chair to greet him. "Drystan! How are ye? I'm so pleased to see ye again, though it will only be for a short bit. I'm going on patrol in a few more days."

He gave her a squeezing bear hug and asked, "Patrol? *My* sister? Ye are enjoying going out with the others to scout out the English?" After the squeeze, he stepped back and gazed at his sister, his hands still gripping her shoulders. "Ye look lovely as ever, Thea, so it must agree with ye. Where have ye gone?"

She filled him in on the last few patrols, making sure to explain all the matchups between the cousins. "But what about ye, Drystan? How do ye fare? Have ye met anyone? Surely there must be a Grant lass who interests ye."

"There are a few, but I have not attached myself to anyone yet. Connor keeps me verra busy."

A voice called to them both from outside. "Is that my son's voice I hear? If so, ye must come outside and see what I'm building."

"Och, Da is calling. Where is Mama?" Drystan asked.

"She's outside with Da. Go see them. I'm preparing the stew for this eve. Never fear—we have plenty."

"More than that for me!" he called as he headed out the door.

She chuckled at her brother. He had one of the biggest appetites ever.

The day passed quickly and the very next morning, Thea challenged Drystan to their usual race in the meadow, something they'd done often when they were younger. At one time, they'd even set up a course that included jumps, poles to circle, and tree branches to duck under. Her mare had been much better at the obstacle course than Drystan's horse, which preferred to snort or buck at whatever obstacle it didn't like.

Now they were happy just to run freely. There was no snow or ice on the ground, so they set out early in the morn in case the weather worsened later in the day. It was such a lovely day that she'd brought Bo and Gerland with her. If their ferociously wagging tails were any indication, they enjoyed the race more than Thea's horse did.

Thea pushed Blossom along, giggling when her sweet mare met the challenge and bolted past her brother, the two deerhounds racing alongside them.

"Come on, Drystan! Ye should be able to keep up."

Her brother was one of her favorite people, along with Lorana. She adored her siblings, and she missed him more than she expected once he'd gone to train with Connor. She loved to tease her brother into racing.

"Go faster! Ye canno' tell me that all those Grants didnae push yer drive to compete. They must have." Drystan had never enjoyed competing, unlike almost everyone she knew.

Aunt Gwyneth and Uncle Logan pushed everyone to compete, but Drystan was just not preoccupied with the thought. He always replied the same way. "Ye know I like to stay in the back and prefer to watch ye all race."

But as his sister, she couldn't help but taunt him. She had enough competitive drive deep inside her for both of them, especially racing across the meadow.

She slowed her mount and leaned toward her brother when he caught up. "Ye know I canno' help myself. Let's go again!"

Blossom felt her small movement and took off like a deer being chased by hunters.

"Be careful, Thea! Ye are on the edge of Ramsay land, and the local patrol just headed back to the castle."

The Ramsay guards on patrol had passed right by the meadow, chattering and challenging her as they crossed her path, laughing at Drystan because he was behind her. Always in the back.

She laughed as she pulled Blossom up again, enjoying the memories of their past races and the fun they'd always had.

But this day was different. Something poked her shoulder, and she jerked around, expecting to see a branch sticking out of her mantle, but there was nothing there. What the hell had just happened?

"Thea! Attack! Run!" Drystan called frantically.

She whirled around instinctively instead of running away, moving toward him to assist in any way she could. Drystan was flanked by two horses, the riders appearing to be Englishmen instead of Scots. They wore dirty garb, no plaids or anything else to identify a clan.

"Drystan, I'm coming," she shouted, grabbing her bow and nocking an arrow so quickly that she didn't even think about what Drystan had said until he shouted at her again.

"Run! Get help."

She couldn't leave her brother. And suddenly there was so much chaos that she didn't know what to do first.

Bo and Gerland went into attack mode, just as they'd been trained to do by Torrian. She loosed her arrow and caught one of the attackers in his shoulder. He bellowed, turning to face her.

The bastard looked familiar. Could it be the same man? The same one who'd tried to kill the fawn?

"Get the hell out of here, Thea. Ride to the

keep for help!" Drystan's sword struck the other man in the leg but her brother made the mistake of looking at her.

That gave his attacker the opportunity to strike Drystan, hitting him broadside with the flat of his sword. Her brother flew off his mount, his horse falling next to him.

"Drystan!"

She nocked another arrow and fired but missed this time. Frantic with the need to be accurate, she couldn't focus or calm herself. She knew it was too important—but her panic prevented her from aiming properly.

This was her brother. She couldn't lose her brother.

Tears blurred her vision and anger shot through her veins. She let out a loud growl at the attackers.

Drystan managed to get back on his horse and reengaged with the marauder. The clash of swords echoed through the air. Drystan struck his attacker in the belly, knocking him off balance, and the man took his horse down with him.

Unfortunately, that horse kicked out, knocking Drystan's horse off balance as well. The poor beast tossed Drystan in the air just before it bolted into the woods, leaving her brother without a mount.

"Get to the keep, Thea!" He went after the man on the ground, but Thea couldn't watch any longer.

The man she'd injured was still on horseback, and he headed directly for her, bellowing. "I'm going to kill you, bitch!"

She'd heard that voice and that accent before. It

was as though she were living through the same fight they'd had on patrol.

Three men that first time, and now only two. But one man was the same, and he was English. She swore it was the same man who'd stepped out to take the fawn and who'd shot that wild arrow over her head. Thea forced herself to calm down enough to nock another arrow, but her hands shook, and her shot went wild this time.

Bo and Gerland turned away from Drystan and came after her attacker, one on either side of him, their deep barking unsettling the man's horse.

Fear coursed through her, and she finally did the one thing she should have done from the start. She sent her horse straight for Ramsay Castle. It was a distance away, but hopefully someone had heard something or suspected there was a problem and would be coming this way.

There was a chance the patrol had heard something and turned back. She could send them to Drystan's aid.

The man caught up with her faster than she would have guessed, still yelling. "You stupid bitch. You'll pay for wounding me." His voice carried a tone that set her on edge, a frantic, threatening tone that said if he ever caught her, she would regret it.

She couldn't put any distance between them, instead hearing him get closer and closer until he finally leaped off his horse and knocked into her, the two of them hurtling through the air. She landed with a thud, the wind gusting out of her as he pinned her.

He landed on top of her, but as soon as she could get a breath, she screamed. A moment later, Bo and Gerland launched themselves at him. One bit his arm and the other his leg, pulling him from her. She reached for the dagger in her boot but froze.

The man stabbed Bo, her hound's yelp ripping her heart in two.

First Drystan and now her dear pet.

"Ye hurt my dog." She reached for Bo but he crawled away, crying in pain. Gerland was more confused than she was. "Run, Gerland. Find Torrian." Gerland took off, barking and racing toward the keep.

The fist to her face got her attention. "I'm going to torture you, bitch. You can suck me off too. Then I'll kill you slowly."

The last comment brought her back to her own perilous situation. She kicked the man between his legs, his howl giving her a moment to push away, but he grabbed her plait and yanked her backward.

He set his face close to hers, close enough that she could see the jagged slice near his eyes from one of the dogs. The blood dripped down the side of his face. "I'll kill your dog first, then I'll deal with you. You are not getting away this time."

He dragged her behind him and moved toward Bo, but she swung her fists, catching him in the side of the head. He reeled back, punching her again.

A growl sounded from behind her.

CHAPTER NINE

WILLUM SHOT UP from his cozy space in the bedchamber, but he had no idea why. Halting in the dark of the night, he held his breath to give him the time he needed to assess the situation.

Something was wrong but he had no idea what. He reached for his sword, gripping it with one hand while his other hand wiped the sweat from his face.

It was the middle of winter and he was sweating. That meant something.

His mother's even breathing came to him, so he knew she was hale.

His father's whisper cut through the night from the other bedchamber. "What's wrong?"

"I dinnae know. Something. I'll go out and check," he whispered back. He donned his boots quickly and stepped outside into the cool air, pausing for any signs of an attack. Would it be a boar or a reiver?

He strolled about with no specific path, walking as quietly as possible to check the area. What had caused him to wake up in the middle of a deep sleep? There wasn't much snow, only a wee bit in well-shaded areas. It wasn't a storm or other weather event that had awakened him.

What the hell?

He took care of his needs, then did a careful canvas of the area, searching for anything unusual, but his exploration revealed nothing.

His father followed him out of the cottage. "Did ye find anything?"

"Nay. Naught." His gaze perused the area again, looking for anything unusual. He whistled for his falcon, and Blue appeared overhead in no time. The bird didn't show signs of any disturbance in the wider area, so Willum shrugged.

Then it hit him. A sensation deep in his gut pressed him, one he couldn't ignore. "Thea's in trouble."

"'Tis the middle of the night."

"I just have this sudden urge to see if she is hale. I was going to leave at dawn anyway. Blue will guide me. I'm going to take my leave, Da. Say goodbye to Mama and apologize for my abrupt leave, will ye?"

"I will." His father caught his gaze, a bit of surprise there. "Ye have strong feelings for Thea."

He thought for a moment, then decided perhaps it was time to be completely honest. "I do, but I dinnae know if anything will come of it. 'Tis too new. Either way, I feel the need to go to her."

His sire clasped his shoulder and said, "Godspeed. We'll stop at Cameron land. If ye need to get in touch with us, we'll be there for a sennight or more."

Willum left right away, mounting his horse and heading to Ramsay land. Blue soared above him. Unable to think through his need to go to Thea's aid, he tried to reason out what might have caused his intense reaction.

It was highly unlikely that she was in trouble at that moment because it was not yet dawn. She should be sound asleep. Dyna often said when she sensed trouble, it was happening at the same time as the event, so this made no sense.

Of course, his aunt Molly had often talked about being able to see things that were to happen in the future. Could that be the situation? Was something bad going to happen to Thea in the hours to come?

He didn't know, but it seemed to take him forever to get there. The closer he came to Ramsay land, the more his palms dampened. Then his back, his neck, his forehead were all drenched with sweat. But night became daylight, so he could see finally where he was headed and who else was about.

The closer he came, the more his skin began to crawl. Something was amiss on Ramsay land, and he had to pray that it did not involve Thea.

He'd just crossed the border of Ramsay land, marked by two trees on either side of the path, when he heard a scream and a dog yelping in pain.

He pushed his horse into a gallop, allowing the sound of the scream to guide him in the right direction. He noticed a few horses flying down the path from the castle, still a distance away, but converging on the source of the scream. He thought it was Torrian, Kyle, Gavin, and a slew of wolfhounds.

Gerland was in the lead. That did not bode well.

Where was Bo and worse—where was Thea?

"Thea?" he yelled, but didn't see anything, The path he was following went through the middle of the forest, so it was not a clear view. He passed by a clearing and rounded a bend in time to see a man put his fist in Thea's face as he dragged her across the ground.

The same man they'd seen on patrol.

Willum's anger burst inside him so quickly that he had to force himself to maintain enough composure to do the right thing, just as his sire had taught him. He fought through the anger and fear as he jumped off his horse and launched himself at the bastard who held Thea.

He had no idea who her assailant was, but he must have been a complete fool, because as soon as he caught sight of Willum and the horses approaching across the meadow from the castle, he let go of Thea and fled. He leapt onto his horse and took off in the opposite direction.

Thea charged after him, but Willum caught her up with an arm around her waist. He spoke to her as softly as he could.

"Nay, ye'll no' catch him on foot. Torrian is coming and he'll get him. Ye need tending."

"Nay, Bo!" She burst into sobs as she pulled away from him to rush to the injured dog lying on the ground panting. Gerland arrived in the next moment, the other dogs right behind him. Her dog pushed his nose into her face for a moment then took up position next to Bo. He was Thea's guard, if Willum were to guess.

"Bo, nay..." She reached for her pet just as Torrian bounded from his horse.

"Careful, Thea. If he's hurt, he could bite. I'll tend him." His gaze took in Thea's disheveled appearance. "Who did this?"

Thea fell back against Willum, sobbing, shaking, looking about her like a cornered animal. "Where is Drystan?"

"We found Drystan. He's fine. Who did this?" Torrian asked again.

Willum had seen the fool and thought he recognized him. "I think 'twas the same man we met on patrol, but he headed toward the main path to get off yer land. Dark-haired, bloody, on a gray speckled horse."

"He's a bloody Englishman," Thea cursed. "He hurt my dog. Torrian, will he live?"

"It looks to be a shallow wound, Thea, but I'm more worried about ye." Torrian looked at Willum. "Get her to Brenna. I'll take Bo to Bethia."

"Nay, I wish to go with him. With ye. Please, Torrian." Her tears wracked Willum's insides as much as they wracked her body. Thea's fears went straight to his heart. He had to do something for her. He would do anything.

But Torrian would brook no argument. "Absolutely no', Thea. Yer presence, in the state ye are in right now, would only distress the dogs. I will take Bo to yer mother, and she will care for him. If ye are there, both dogs will focus on ye. That will delay their healing and yers." He motioned for Willum to get her moving while he dealt with the dogs. "I'll find yer horse, Thea. And Drystan's. Get yerself to Brenna. Ye are bleeding and swelling as ye speak."

Willum set her on his horse sideways, then climbed up behind her so his arms would be on either side of her, keeping her secure. She leaned against him sobbing so hard that she was unable to speak.

As soon as he turned his horse around, Torrian gave Willum his last piece of advice. "Find out what ye can. Take in all ye see along the way. Gavin will go along with ye. Kyle will stay with me."

As soon as they were a short distance away, Thea said, "Turn around. Forget what Torrian said. We're going after that rotten bastard, Willum."

He'd been wrong before; he would not do anything for her. Even though he was falling in love with her, his next words would surely make her hate him.

CHAPTER TEN

"NAY, THEA. YE will see a healer first."
Thea didn't hear that stern tone often
from Willum. "Turn around. He's getting away."
She had to make the bastard pay for hurting
her dog. But she wasn't accustomed to feeling
so weak, and she fell against Willum's firm chest.
A sudden exhaustion overpowered her, and she
grabbed onto his forearm to steady herself.

Another group of guards on horseback shot
past them, and Gavin pointed them in the right
direction.

As soon as they passed, Gavin pulled abreast of
them. "Ye are going nowhere, Thea Douglas, and
ye know it. I know ye love yer dog, but if ye saw
yer face at present, ye would probably agree with
us. Ye will see yer grandmother first."

"Who else has returned besides Grandda?"
Willum asked.

"Aye, all have returned," Gavin replied. "Da is
starting to pace already. Stories of the English in
Berwick Castle are spreading quickly. Patrol will
be leaving soon, and ye must be ready, Thea. Ye
and the others are needed by King Robert."

Thea swallowed, doing her best to calm her racing heart after all that had happened. More and more Ramsay guards passed them, going in the opposite direction. One horse stopped and her great uncle's voice called out to her. "Stop, MacLerie. I need to ask her questions."

"Nay, we move on. She needs Aunt Brenna."

Uncle Logan called out from behind them. "Did ye just refuse me, MacLerie? Stop him, Gavin."

"Da," Gavin roared, "she's injured! Find Drystan for yer answers or follow the guards who are after the bastard. Willum made the right choice. If ye wish to ask her any questions, it will wait until Aunt Brenna gives permission."

Uncle Logan grumbled and declared, "'Tis most unlikely to happen anytime soon. That woman is a stubborn tyrant. I'll ride next to ye."

Willum did not stop but urged his mount into an easy jog. He held Thea tightly, for which she was grateful. This man was as steadfast as anyone. Her mother and father would be frantic, but she was fine.

Or so she thought.

Uncle Logan rode alongside them. "English or Scots?"

Her gaze found her uncle and focused on his face. As coarse as he sounded, she knew he loved her, and he'd chase the bastard down as fast as anyone. She didn't bother to lift her head from where it rested against Willum's shoulder. She was quickly losing her strength, so she wrapped both arms around Willum's waist to keep herself from falling.

"He was English," Willum said. "I saw him. I think it was the same man who we ran into on patrol setting traps for deer. When we came along and set a fawn free, he fired at us then, furious we interfered."

"One of Edward's men?"

"Nay. There were only two attackers and not in any uniform." Willum hadn't seen the other attacker, but he'd heard about Drystan's troubles from Gavin as they rode.

"Did the bastard touch ye, Thea?" Uncle Logan asked, his voice a tone of barely controlled fury she'd not heard often from him.

Again Willum answered for her. "He punched her. Her face is swelling." He pulled his arm back enough so her uncle could see the damage to her face.

Finally she found her voice. "He punched me, said he was going to torture me, make me pay."

"Pay for what?" Uncle Logan asked.

"The arrow I put in his shoulder and letting the fawn go," she said, the hitching in her breath starting again. "But after I struck his shoulder, after I saw Drystan fighting the other man, I couldn't aim anymore. He looked like the same man to me also. I was so upset that my hands shook. I missed every other shot." The tears returned at the thought of how she'd failed her brother.

"'Twas good work to hit one of them, lass," Willum said.

"We'll hunt him down. Have nae fear." Her great uncle barked out every word, his anger evident in his tone.

Uncle Logan left and Gavin took the lead.

Willum kissed her forehead. She snuggled closer.

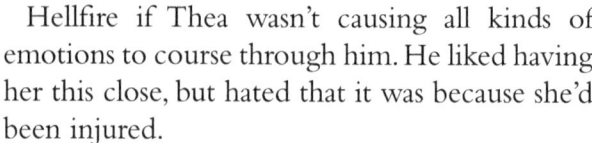

Hellfire if Thea wasn't causing all kinds of emotions to course through him. He liked having her this close, but hated that it was because she'd been injured.

He had a powerful need for vengeance against the man who dared to hurt her—who dared to touch her. If his sire were standing in front of him, he'd tell him that he knew his purpose now. It was threefold.

Love Thea.

Protect Thea.

Kill the bastard who'd hurt her.

The gates of Ramsay Castle were quickly opened for their small group, and Gavin motioned for Willum to take his mount straight to the steps of the keep. Chaos reigned everywhere, but he ignored it. Thea's eyes were closed so he handed her down to Gavin, then took her back into his arms when someone called for Gavin.

Worried for a moment about how he was going to open the door, he needn't have. A group of castle residents followed him, clearly concerned, and one retainer cleared the way to Brenna's healing chamber for him.

He set her down carefully onto the cot indicated by his great aunt Brenna Ramsay, Thea's grandmother.

"Has she been speaking to ye, Willum?"

"Aye, Aunt Brenna. She was completely lucid, worried about her dog, crying frequently. She fell asleep right before we arrived. She'll be fine, do ye no' think so?" He reached for her hand, rubbing his over her cold skin. Her skin looked ashen, her long dark lashes a stark contrast.

"Thea," Aunt Brenna tapped her cheek. "Come now. Ye must awaken for me. I wish to ask ye some questions. Wake up for a few moments."

The door opened, and Thea's father barreled inside. "Where is she? Is she hale?"

He took one look at his daughter and collapsed onto a nearby stool. "What happened? I know no' what all has happened, but I'm ill with worry. Drystan was attacked, Bo has been stabbed, and my wee lass looks as though someone put a fist into her face." He looked to Willum. "Do ye know what happened?"

Thea's eyes fluttered open, and Aunt Brenna sat on the bed next to her, cocooning her hands in hers. "Wake up, lass. I must know what happened. Yer face took the worst of it, I believe, but I must hear it from ye."

"Why isn't she answering?" Donnan asked.

"Sometimes the events of an attack are so shocking to a person that they have to go inside to maintain control. Not the medical explanation, but 'tis how I've seen it after all these years. They're stunned by the activities and sleep a wee bit to heal themselves from the inside. I dinnae see any large amount of blood as evidence of a cut."

Thea's eyes opened and locked on Willum's, then her sire's. "Drystan. Da, where is Drystan?"

Her father said, "He's fine, Thea. One small cut. And yer mama is stitching Bo up. She said the wound is shallow and no' to worry. I wish to know who did this to ye. Did ye know them?"

She nodded, and Aunt Brenna's hand reached over to Donnan's hand. "Donnan, why do ye no' talk to Willum outside while I tend Thea."

Donnan looked up at him, then leaned over to kiss Thea's forehead. He motioned for Willum to go into the hall with him. As they stepped out, a group came in from outside. Torrian led the way, his tunic covered in blood from the dog, followed by Kyle, Grandda, and Uncle Gavin. The chieftain motioned the group over to a nearby trestle table, and they settled there, Donnan and Willum joining them.

How Willum admired Torrian for the job he did as chieftain. The man always stayed calm and was able to make decisions quicker than a rabbit on the run.

"We were unable to find the man who accosted Thea," Torrian said, grimacing in regret. "We questioned the man who Drystan fought with, managing to get some answers before he took his last breath. None of Drystan's blows were fatal; I believe the man's horse fell on him and shattered his pelvis. At first, he didnae wish to answer, but I was able to convince him."

Willum could guess how the man had managed to get answers, but he wouldn't ask.

Torrian continued. "They are from a group of men hired to fight in the Lowlands for King Edward. They came from England and were told in the Borderlands that Scots were easy to steal from, and since the famine is affecting them greatly, they were in search of anything they could steal or eat. They were hoping for horses and had seen the patrol all on horseback so they followed them here. Willum, ye saw them before?"

"Aye. They were setting traps for deer and caught a fawn. Thea set it free, but that angered them and they fired at us. There were three of them but I hit one in the leg with my arrow. He said they sought vengeance for what Thea did." Slimy bastards going after a woman like they had. It fired up his own need for revenge for hurting Thea.

Torrian said, "He also said they'd never seen a woman use a bow before. Thea caught them by surprise."

"Did ye get a name?" Willum asked. He prayed he had some way of finding the man who hurt Thea.

"I did. Fulke Slater he called him. From York. He said they were heading to Berwick Castle from here. King Edward will be arriving within a moon.

Willum tipped his head sideways, locking the name into his mind.

Fulke Slater.

He was going hunting for a man named Fulke.

CHAPTER ELEVEN

THEA DIDN'T HAVE any trouble waking up once her grandmother found her some warm broth to drink. She sat up while the sweet woman poked and prodded her relentlessly.

"I'm fine, Grandmama." She took another long sip of the broth, allowing the warm brew to stay in her mouth for a bit before swallowing it.

"Ye may think so, but ye must calm yerself. Ye are riled because yer pet is hurt and ye watched Drystan battle. He's capable, trained by one of the best in all the land, so ye must put yer worry about him off to the side. Ye will heal quicker if ye arenae upset. Tell me about Bo," Grandmama instructed, poking at Thea's face. Thea winced a few times as certain spots were pressed.

"Ow," she muttered, a bit embarrassed she couldn't stop herself from complaining.

"It hurts? How badly?"

"Just a wee bit. 'Tis the spot near my cheekbone that hurts the most."

"Bo?" her grandmother prompted, getting up from her stool to mix a potion.

"The villain stabbed him, though Torrian thinks it is a shallow wound."

Her grandmother turned to her with a wide smile. "And ye know ye have the best in all the land to tend to him. Are ye learning yer mother's ways so ye can help her when she gets older?"

Not as much as she should be, but the question did make her think. What would they all do if anything happened to prevent her mother from tending all their animals?

"I trust yer mother will fix Bo. And Gerland is fine?"

"Aye."

"Here, drink this. 'Twill take away some of yer pain."

"I dinnae wish to sleep."

"Ye have my word that I've just put in enough to numb the pain a bit. Should ye wish for something to help ye sleep in the next few days, come find me and I'll give ye a stronger potion. Now I must ask ye. Were ye hurt in any place that I canno' see? Did he attempt to molest ye?" Grandmama sat on the stool and gazed straight into Thea's eyes.

She shook her head. "He wished to, but he didnae get the opportunity." Her grandmother was the sweetest person alive, she thought, though her mother was nearly as sweet. How she adored both of them. Being this close to her grandmother made her realize how much the two looked alike. Their eyes were the same shade of brown, filled with enough compassion and wisdom to cause her to wish to have just a wee bit of what they both had.

But she didn't. Drystan and Lorana were more like her mother. She favored her father. "May I go? I'd like to see how Bo is doing."

"Aye." Her grandmother leaned down and placed a kiss on the top of her head. "Ye may take yer leave as long as ye have someone with ye. Have yer sire or Willum go with ye. I dinnae think ye have any permanent damage, but yer face will be sore for a few days. And ye shall see so many colors of the rainbow that ye'll think ye will never be the same again." She patted her hand and then moved over to the center table. "When is patrol leaving?"

"Either the morrow or the next day." She climbed out of the bed and set her clothing to rights.

"I hope no' until the next day."

"I must go, Grandmama."

She whirled around to face Thea and put her hands on her hips. "Ye will no' go looking for the bastard. 'Twill gain ye nothing. Ye will patrol as Maitland and Dyna instruct ye. Promise me ye willnae go off on yer own, lass."

Thea rolled her eyes.

"Dinnae roll yer eyes like Isla does. I hate it."

"Sorry, Grandmama." She let out a deep sigh. "I am grateful ye will allow me to patrol, and of course I will only do as our leaders wish. I wouldnae go against them."

"And dinnae think of convincing them that

ye must chase after this man. Did he take any injuries?"

"Aye, I put an arrow in his shoulder."

"Then know that he could be dead in a few days. He'll rip the arrow out, and it will surely fill with the green poison and kill him because he'll no' go to a healer. Forget about the one man. Vengeance will no' serve ye well. I've seen it destroy some."

"I promise to follow their instructions." She stood and made her way to the side of the door.

"Good. Please stop and see me before the patrol leaves so I know ye are healing the way ye should be." Her grandmother bent over her jars of poultices and ointments, fussing as she often did, brushing her gray hairs back from her face. Her shoulders were beginning to round a wee bit, a sign of advancing age. Thea didn't wish to ever live without the dear woman, and she refused to think on it.

The door opened and Dyna entered. "Ye are hale?" Thea nodded, and Dyna raised her voice so her grandmother would hear her question. "She can go on patrol with us, Aunt Brenna?"

"She may go, but only if she does no' chase after the one who punched her. When are ye leaving?"

"One more day. Our plan is for a longer journey, nearly a moon this time. King Edward is headed to Berwick Castle, and King Robert wishes to gain it back. We'll be traveling between Berwick and Edinburgh to protect our people. We'll have no time to chase a rogue Englishman."

"Good," her grandmother said. "A rogue who could be lying on the ground somewhere fighting the fever. He'll probably lose the battle, so no reason to search for him."

Dyna looked at Thea, her hands on her hips. "Canno' argue that reasoning. We head straight south. No distractions, Thea. And we have a full group. Eight of us."

"Who?" Grandmama asked. "Besides Maitland, Willum and ye two. That's four. Alaric is here and I hear Eli is going. Who am I missing?"

"Tevis and Wenna."

"A fine group. Thea must check with me before she goes, Dyna. I wish to see her healing well. I'll see ye tomorrow eve, lass."

"I promise, Grandmama." She kissed her grandmother's cheek and left with Dyna.

Dyna whispered, "Dinnae worry, we'll find him."

"But I promised not to," Thea explained.

Dyna grinned. "But I didn't."

Two days later, Thea lifted Bo and settled him in her lap, not a light task for certes. He was heavy and awkward like most deerhounds, everything about him long and lanky. He was still on the mend, but thanks to her mother's fine skills, his wound was healing and his tail had begun to wag again. It pleased her even more that he was able to stand long enough to do what he needed to do.

Gerland came forward and licked her cheek as

she snuggled Bo, rubbing him behind the ear just the way he liked it.

"Worry not, laddies. I shall return. We have business to take care of."

Her parents came out of the cottage. Lorana remained inside. It was always difficult for her sister to see her leave. Drystan had left for Grant land the day before, returning to his lessons. That meant Lorana would be alone with her parents and would be spoiled, for certes.

"Thea, will ye leave the revenge to others, if ye please?" Her father said as he reached her. "I wish no' to worry overmuch about ye." He wrapped his arm around her mother's shoulders.

"Thea, please promise me." Her mother leaned her head into her husband's embrace.

"Mama, ye know I'll behave. There are eight of us, and we have work to do. I'll no' have time to chase the phantom. I wish to never see the man again." She kissed Bo's head and his tail thumped against her leg.

She set the animal down and moved over to give her parents a big hug. "Dinnae worry about me. I'll be fine. We have a grand group, and we'll all protect each other. I saw Grandmama last eve, and she said I was healing fine. She gave me a potion to take along just in case. Take care of Bo and Gerland, and I'll be back in about a fortnight as ye wished, but if anything happens, no more than a moon."

Her father kissed her forehead. "Ye look worse now than before, shades of purple and blue mixed with yellow. Ye must be mighty sore, lass."

"I'm fine, Da." As long as she didn't touch her face, it didn't hurt. Her occasional headache could be cured by her grandmother's potion. Headaches in the woods on patrol could prove to be brutal.

Her mother handed her a sack of food to take along, and she grabbed her bag full of extra clothing and other small items, attaching both to her saddle. Her father gave her a boost onto her horse just as the others approached.

Dyna waved to her parents. "We'll take good care of her, Bethia. I promise. And we shall return for reinforcements if need be. We hope to take Berwick Castle back. King Robert has hoped to gain it back for a long time. If successful, we shall return to celebrate."

Her mother brushed a tear away, and Thea said, "Da, ye'll have to hold Gerland back. Ye know he'll try to follow, but he canno'."

"We'll keep them both here. Dinnae worry."

"We head to Edinburgh first," Maitland said. "We hope to meet King Robert there, since the English still hold Berwick Castle."

"Godspeed!" her parents called out in unison.

The group headed down the path toward the main road south, riding two abreast. Thea rode next to Eli. "Are ye excited to be on yer first patrol?"

"Hellfire, but I surely am!" she nearly shouted.

Alaric, who rode in front of them, turned around. "Are what?"

"Happy to be on patrol," she replied.

"Ye cursed about being on patrol?"

"Ye have a problem with a lass cursing, Grant?" Eli's gaze narrowed at Alaric. If Thea were to guess, the young woman was hoping for an argument. Eli loved verbal sparring as much as physical. Her chestnut-brown hair fell to her waist and was tightly plaited. Thea thought her one of the prettiest in the clan, but she made no attempt to attract men.

Alaric narrowed his gaze at Eli and said, "Nay. Just curious. Curse all ye like, lass." He returned his gaze to the front, beginning a conversation with Willum.

"He thinks because he's good-looking that everyone likes him. Mayhap no'."

Thea laughed. "He might hear ye."

Willum was not directly in front of her, so she could see his face, and she noticed him grin and cast a sideways glance toward Thea. He'd heard Eli's words, so surely Alaric had also.

Thea couldn't argue with Eli's assessment of the man's looks. Alaric had the fair hair and haunting blue eyes of his mother, Gracie. He wore his hair long to his neck. His long, neatly trimmed beard was a shade darker than his hair.

Alaric was handsome, but she preferred Willum's dark looks. At present, she could see the scruff of Willum's beard starting. He trimmed it perhaps once a fortnight, so he always had a dark shadow.

She liked it. It made her wonder if he had dark hair on his chest or if he was one of those men who had no hair. She wasn't sure which she would prefer. How odd that she would even think about what color and thickness a man's chest hair might be. She'd never done it before.

They entered a meadow and as soon as the field opened up, Eli sent her horse into a full gallop with a whistle, heading off into the distance.

Maitland headed after her, catching up with her in a short time, and Eli's horse slowed. Thea couldn't tell if Eli had stopped because she saw him approaching or if Maitland had grabbed the reins of her horse.

Either way, he stopped Eli from going any farther and waited for the rest of them to catch up. "I realize this is yer first trip with us, Eli, but ye willnae bring attention to us again like that. We are to move swiftly and quietly, so that we see before we are seen. We were accosted on our land by English soldiers, so we must be astute and ready for more since the one marauder swore vengeance against us. The famine has made many hungry, and they will do anything when starvation begins to take them."

Eli, appropriately chastised, blushed and let the rest of the group catch up to her. Maitland waited for them to gather, staying in the center while the others formed a semi-circle around him.

"Ye will all listen carefully. I should have told ye earlier, but I wished to be away from Ramsay land. King Robert has received reports from one of the wardens of the marches that the English are going hungry in Berwick Castle, and ye've all heard the tale of the two English bastards who came to Ramsay land because of it. Edward's men are hungry and looking for cattle and horses.

We will not draw attention to ourselves, and no one—I repeat, no one—is to go off alone. If ye need to take care of yer needs, lasses keep together. But know this—starving men will attack foolishly. Dinnae risk anything. This patrol will be verra different. Be on guard always."

Thea glanced at the others in the group. Were they as surprised as she was?

In her younger days, this warning might have frightened her, but not this day. This day she relished the thought of meeting starving Englishmen.

Especially if one had a wound in his right shoulder.

CHAPTER TWELVE

W ILLUM SUSPECTED THAT this patrol would be different than the others in more ways than Maitland had listed. He knew more than one member of this patrol was out for one English bastard's blood. He'd heard about the first patrol at Carlisle, when Isla and Grif had been thrown together in the dungeon, but he and Wenna had not been here then. Perhaps the next newcomers to Ramsay land would hear tales of this one.

The patrol group headed south without incident until they neared Edinburgh, when they were approached by a few members of Clan Grant.

Willum recognized Loki first, riding at the head of the small group of men. "Maitland, greetings to ye and yer patrol. Are ye interested in sharing a fine meal with us? Dobbin told me we would likely meet up with ye and chat for a bit. There's a fine clearing not far from here. We'll no' be bothered by anyone."

Dyna looked to Maitland and arched a pitiful brow at him. "If ye please? I'm famished."

Maitland nodded his agreement. "I'm hungry and would love something besides an oatcake. And 'twould be good to hear what ye have to tell us about the situation here, Loki."

Loki chuckled. "Ye are always famished, Dyna. We have plenty. I made sure to buy extra. Market day, though as ye know, when it comes to fresh food there's little available. We have plenty of dried meat and bread. We managed to find someone who still had beans, though the price was hefty."

"Wonderful," Maitland said.

Loki was traveling with his son Lucas and his grandson Dobbin. They'd brought three guards with them, as well. The two groups mixed and chatted as Loki led the way to the place they'd scouted.

They reached the clearing, and Dyna was the first off her horse. "Anyone else wish to go with me, ladies? I'm running!"

Thea laughed and hollered, "I'll join ye."

Wenna followed the two of them into the bushes, calling behind her, "Come with us, Eli. Ye canno' go alone out here."

Eli followed, and the four lasses disappeared into the woods.

The men tethered the horses, loosening saddle girths and ensuring they had enough slack in their ties to graze.

"What have ye heard about the English in Berwick Castle?" Maitland asked. "It seems Edward hasnae sent any food and the guards are now on the hunt, going in search of any animals to feed the men there."

Loki fussed with the packages tied to his saddle. "'Tis true. Sir James Douglas is still patrolling the area closest to Berwick because he's warden in the area. We happened to meet up with him before we arrived in Edinburgh. A few of the English protecting the castle sneak out occasionally in a sad attempt to find food, but he's no' seen any return. He's guessing they die from starvation or fever or are caught in the act. Meeting Douglas was a boon to our trip—we've been more alert for any news we can take back to Grant Castle. Our only intent was to shop for my daughter. Ami wanted new fabric for clothing so here we are."

Dobbin drawled, "Ami always gets what she wants. New boots too."

Lucas asked, "What are ye wearing on yer feet, Dobbin?"

"But I really needed them. She has two pairs."

Loki waved his grandson away and sat on a log in the clearing, a sack full of packages wrapped in twine piled in front of him.

"Ye have enough to share? There are eight of us, Loki. Though my belly feels like it has room for food for two." Maitland chuckled.

"Sympathy for yer wife's bigger belly?"

"Aye. True. I admit I'm excited about the prospect of our laddie."

"Ye sure 'twill be a lad?"

"Aye, we both feel it."

"Here's our largest loaf of bread. Share it amongst ye and I'll pass the sack full of apples around. They are no' the freshest, but I was surprised to find any. Someone had them in cold storage since autumn. Then I have some chicken legs that were smoked not long ago."

Willum sat down next to Maitland, Alaric next to him. "Chicken legs. Yum. Anything but rabbit makes me happy."

As they shared the food around, the lasses returned and Dobbin started a fire for them all to gather around.

Maitland tossed the bare bone of a chicken leg into the fire. "King Robert wishes for us to keep the English in the Borderlands and trapped in Berwick until he takes the castle back. Where are we needed most? Have ye heard?"

"A group of soldiers in disguise headed into Edinburgh, begging for food so I'm told. Douglas said to find them and send them out. We couldnae locate them. Ye can try. They say they are split into two groups of five. They are stealing anything they can: food, coin, livestock. Anything they can sell or eat. And I'm told they are gaunt. They are hungry and desperate. I wish ye luck. I suggest ye search the outskirts of the city and check the taverns at night. Ye might catch them. If ye do, bring them to Douglas. He'll handle them."

Willum had to admit the thought of this tactic made his skin crawl. He didn't wish to go inside any tavern, since they were often filled with unwashed men wall-to-wall. That was exactly the type of situation that could make him lose his head.

Crowds in tight spaces.

Being alone in the woods.

His two biggest fears. With eight of them, he needn't worry about being alone, especially with Maitland's rules about always traveling in pairs.

But he didn't like the idea of Edinburgh. Any burgh made his insides curdle from distaste.

Loki and his group took their leave after the meal, heading back into the Highlands.

"Dyna, let's no' waste any time," Maitland said. "If we're looking for English thieves in Edinburgh, then we should find a place to sleep this eve. We'll split up. Choose yer team and we'll get on our way."

"I'll take Thea, Alaric, and Willum. Work for ye?"

"Aye, off to Edinburgh. There are two inns I know where the questionable oft shelter. I'll take the worst of the two places. Ye take the other."

Willum let out a breath. He was more than pleased to have Thea with him.

Perhaps he'd get the chance to steal a kiss. A real one.

They'd spent three days in Edinburgh and hadn't met an Englishman anywhere. The entire group was to meet on the morrow to decide whether to stay or go elsewhere.

Thea rode next to Willum as they headed for dinner at the inn they were staying at. The closer they came, the more Willum acted unusually strange.

"Willum, is everything all right?"

He shook his head, then nodded, a contradiction of its own, one that told her he was not his usual agreeable self.

"What's bothering ye?" He may not trust her enough yet to tell her the truth, but she had to ask. Something was definitely upsetting his usual calm demeanor.

"Naught. I'm fine," he replied, glancing at her but scratching his head, then rubbing his beard, his hand going down his neck before scratching his arm.

She had an inkling what was wrong but had no idea how to help him. "The inn. 'Tis what's bothering ye. Ye need to be out in the open. Ye've slept inside for three nights and the fourth one is coming this eve."

His gaze nearly brought her to tears. She'd said it perfectly, if she were to guess, because he looked as pleased as anything, just because she understood.

"'Tis fine, Willum. I dinnae see why ye and Alaric canno' sleep out under the stars."

"Ye have the right of it, and I commend ye for it. 'Tis exactly how I'm feeling. But I'll no' sleep outside with ye two lasses inside."

"We can handle ourselves. We are in the same bedchamber." They'd been fortunate to get the largest chamber the inn had. It even had a table and four chairs, large enough that they used it to discuss the patrol when necessary.

"Nay, I couldnae sleep knowing ye were in there and I was so far from all of ye. But that I've learned to handle in our room at the inn. Once I fall asleep, 'tis no problem at all." He scratched his head again. So something still bothered him.

"Then what has ye unsettled?"

"'Tis the dining hall. I believe the morrow is market day, which brings more people to Edinburgh and more to the inns."

"Ah, ye are correct. Market day is on the morrow, and the inn will be full." The inn had been quiet for the evening meal the last two nights, but she was sure this night and the next would be raucous and crowded.

"I wish we could leave, but we canno', because if the English are going to return, 'tis most likely to be on market day."

"'Struth. More people, more food, more coin. More crowds, more chances to steal." She didn't wish to tell him that she overheard Maitland and Dyna discussing the fact that James Douglas believed the English in Berwick Castle were so hungry that they were headed in this direction— intent on market day. Willum was wise enough to figure this out on his own. And he had already.

"More ways to steal and hide. If they are to be found, I understand that the morrow is the most likely day."

Thea thought on the reasoning, unable to find much to discount the truth they both uncovered, except for one thing. "Why here instead of Carlisle or a smaller town in the Borderlands?"

"Because the famine of last summer affected the Borderlands most of all. They say the English at Berwick Castle are eating their horses to survive.

In the Highlands, the rain that wouldn't let up did not sit on our land. We have natural run-off for the heavy rain, so though our crops struggled and some were swept away, at least they didn't rot in the fields. But ye know it has been difficult for all of us. The Ramsay cook is always cursing."

"The Grant stores helped us. They had a large supply of seed well hidden. Do ye know my sire began to build boxes for planting above the ground as the rains continued? He had his own wee farm behind our house. If not, we would have been without any harvest at all."

"Yer sire is a clever man."

"So they come to steal food, but will the market have much to sell?"

"Nay, ye'll not see much other than meat, and even the cows are smaller. Those boars we killed on our last patrol were half the size of any we hunted last year. Aunt Brenna hoards salt, and that has been a blessing."

They arrived at the inn, and Thea paused, glancing up and down the street. It was full of patrons, peasants, and sellers heading to market. "They are readying for the morrow so soon?"

"Some will sell tonight, is my guess. Sell what little they have so they can buy from the stands before they sell out of product. This will be most difficult."

Thea noticed how sweat broke out on his forehead, letting her know exactly how difficult this was for him. She had to find a way to help him through this evening, which was sure to be torture for him.

"Willum, I can go inside and tell Dyna we wish to eat outside."

"Nay, we must study the people inside, and I fear if we are outside, the food will be plucked from our verra hands. At least, we can survey the crowd inside and out, then take our food above stairs to eat."

He took the reins of her horse and led her to the stable yard behind the inn. They'd paid enough coin to feed and stable the horses at the inn, an exorbitant expense, but a necessary one. He had to wonder if the horses were given oats, hay, or just kitchen scraps. No matter. Hopefully, they'd be on their way to a different site on the morrow.

He reached for Thea's waist just as Dyna and Alaric arrived behind them.

"Hellfire, but 'tis too large a crowd in the streets this eve. Why?" Dyna asked.

"Market day, we assumed," Thea replied.

"Not usually this busy, but perhaps."

Alaric settled his mount next to Willum's. "'Tis nearing the end of winter, and there's little food left from last year's harvest. The stores are thinning, even on Grant land. The peasants have little or no food left. There will be plenty of begging and stealing at the market on the morrow."

The group moved into the crowd, and Willum took Thea's hand.

"I can handle myself, Willum. Ye need no' hang on to me."

"I dinnae like this crowd." His gaze narrowed

as he scanned the growing mass of peasants and merchants.

Dyna's expression grew more concerned as they made their way among the mob. "I dinnae like this either. Something is off." She lifted her head but wasn't quite tall enough to see. "I wish I was as tall as my sire."

Alaric turned around, giving her his back. "Come, I'll hoist ye."

Dyna jumped up onto Alaric's back, and he lifted her easily, her head far above the others. She scanned the area, now packed with strangers. "Och, I dinnae like this."

"What is it?" Alaric asked.

Then her eyes widened. "They're here. I knew it."

"Who?" Willum asked.

She pointed down the way. "The English. I could smell them, I swear, but the true sign is their pathetic weapons. Have they no pride in their armorers? I believe I see a group not far down the path. We need to get inside."

Dyna dropped down from Alaric's back and shuffled ahead of him, pushing and shoving people out of the way, the rest of the group following. One man spun around to strike her but she kicked him in the groin and he let her be, howling in the crowd.

No one cared.

Before Thea knew it, she was overcome by the power of the crowd, pushing and shoving, sending her in the wrong direction.

"Get the hell out of my way!" she shouted, but

no one listened. There were twice as many men as women in the street, and she couldn't see over their heads.

She had the sudden urge to hold Willum's hand again so she looked for him.

But he wasn't there.

"Dyna! Willum! Where the hell are ye? Where did ye go?" She searched the crowd in every direction but saw no one she recognized. Body odor, smirking men, hands landing where they didn't belong. She shoved and pushed, but to no avail.

Something struck her in the back of the head and she screamed.

"Thea!" She heard Willum's voice but couldn't answer. Her knees weakened beneath her.

She fought the weakness, but within a few moments, the pain in her head was so strong that she thought she was about to lose consciousness. She scratched at anyone near her and fought to get away from the hand that wrenched her in the opposite direction. But was powerless against the strong pull on her arm. Before she could scream again, she was tossed across the back of a horse, her hands bound and a foul rag stuffed into her mouth. She fought and kicked and received another blow to the head for her trouble. She went limp from pain, and the horse started moving down the path.

Away from the inn.

CHAPTER THIRTEEN

WILLUM'S BELLY ROILED. He could no longer see Thea. She'd been propelled into the middle of the street, and he'd lost her among the sea of bodies.

"Thea!" He called out to her but didn't hear a response.

"Where the hell did she go?" Alaric stood not far from him, scanning the area as he did.

"I dinnae know." He shoved a few obnoxious men to clear them away from him, but he couldn't find her dark brown hair anywhere.

Then he heard her muffled scream.

From a distance too far away to do anything, he spotted Thea, stomach down across a horse, a strange man behind her, a firm grasp on Thea's back. He guided the horse away from the crowd, moving quickly and not caring who his horse trampled.

It was not Fulke Slater. Of that much he was certain. "Dyna!" He pointed toward the horse in the hopes that she could see and would recognize the man stealing Thea away. Though he guessed Dyna was too short to see, he noticed Alaric was doing his best to follow the horse with his gaze. "Can ye see who it is? Do ye see him?"

"I see the back of his head, but nothing about him looks familiar to me. We've got to get a horse and follow." Alaric headed back toward the stable.

Dyna, riding bareback, shot out from behind the inn and took off in the same direction as the fool, but she was too late. The other rider reached an area where the crowd had dispersed, and he sent his mount into a gallop. Dyna's horse had been held up, now surrounded by men shouting in protest. She was less willing to risk injury to innocent bystanders by riding over them.

Willum followed Alaric toward the stable, but they were stopped by the commotion around Dyna. A few of the men were reaching for her now.

Alaric snorted. "They'll all regret that mistake."

"Stay here and keep an eye on Dyna in case she needs help. I'll get our horses." Willum headed behind the inn, knowing that he had to hurry if they were going to have any chance of catching up to Thea. He cursed as he shoved people out of his way, but he made it to the back, pleased to see his horse had been fed and watered.

The crowd began to thin as night descended, giving him the chance to get back onto the street without fighting anyone. In his rush, he followed Dyna's example and didn't fully tack up their mounts. They'd all grown up riding bareback, and time was streaming away.

Alaric mounted, and they reached Dyna, who rolled her eyes and said, "Blasted buffoons."

Willum counted five men with blood dripping from various wounds, but they were smart enough to retreat and now kept well out of reach.

Frantic, Willum asked Dyna, "Where did he take her?"

"Toward the castle. What I feared most. I thought he might be Fulke, but he's wearing a faded brown plaid. No' one I recognize and clearly no' English."

The three headed toward the castle, stopping when they reached the wall around the city.

Willum asked, "Do ye think they went inside?"

"I do," Dyna said. "He took the path straight toward the gate. I couldnae see past the wall to see where he was taking her. Let's find a quiet place to plan." She pointed to a spot down the path, out of the way of the others entering the city, where they could speak without worry of eavesdroppers.

Once they were gathered together again, Dyna explained, "There's a market inside the city too, so we should be able to get inside. But I'd also like Maitland's help. Alaric, will ye go find Maitland and the others at their inn, and meet us near the castle right after nightfall?"

"Where will we meet ye?" Alaric asked. "I've never been inside the wall."

"There's a small inn where they know my sire well, and probably Maitland too. Maitland will know the place. Willum and I will see if we can find Thea while ye get the others. See ye at dark."

"Agreed. We'll leave now," Alaric said. "I hope

the crowd has thinned and Eli and Wenna are fine."

Willum worried about his sister for a moment, but he thought of Maitland and Tevis next to her. They would take care of her so he forced his mind away. At present, he had more important things to worry about.

Thea.

As soon as Alaric left, Dyna's hands went to cocoon the top of her head. She bent over at the waist, her hands still arranged as if she needed to protect her head. Was she having a severe headache?

"Dyna, what's happening? Ye look in pain. Tell me how I can help ye." Distressed wasn't a strong enough word to describe the expression on her face, and it was surely hard to watch her.

Her breathing came in short pants, her hands moving to her knees as she stayed bent over, trying to regain control over whatever overpowered her.

"Dyna?"

As quickly as she'd bent over, she stood erect, nearly knocking into him. "I know where Thea is. She's outside the city walls."

"Still near Edinburgh?"

"Aye. She's in the cellar of a dilapidated castle on the outskirts of the city."

A sprig of hope blossomed inside Willum. "Mayhap she'll get out on her own."

"Nay. She's bound and there are at least two dogs guarding her. We have to move quickly."

Dyna didn't have to tell him twice.

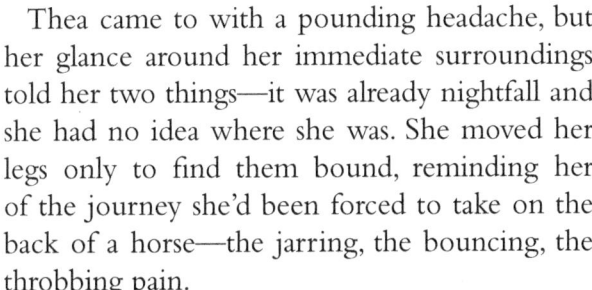

Thea came to with a pounding headache, but her glance around her immediate surroundings told her two things—it was already nightfall and she had no idea where she was. She moved her legs only to find them bound, reminding her of the journey she'd been forced to take on the back of a horse—the jarring, the bouncing, the throbbing pain.

The only thing she knew about the bastard who'd abducted her was that he was a Scot. At first, she'd almost wished that her captor would turn out to be Fulke, but she realized that wasn't the case as soon as she heard his Scottish burr. It had been hard to track where they were going, with her draped across the saddle like a sack, but she remembered stumbling through a back entrance of some old manor home before being forced to drink some potion that made her sleepy.

The last thing she recalled was looking at the man and saying, "Ye will regret this. I'm a Ramsay and my grandmother is Gwyneth Ramsay."

He'd laughed and said, "She's an old goat now. I'll no' worry about her or any other Ramsay, because I'll no' have ye for long. Ye are worth a substantial amount of coin, and I'll have a buyer for ye by the morrow." He'd had a helper who tied her hands and feet together as the awful concoction took effect.

The cot she was on now was small, but at least

she was not on the hard stone of the floor. Stone floors usually indicated a castle of some kind, so perhaps they'd moved out of the manor house she'd been in before. There were embers in the hearth not far away, and she thought she was alone, but then the hair on the back of her neck bristled. She held her breath, and the sound of someone else breathing reached her ears.

A young lad sat in a chair beside the door.

"Ye are awake. Please dinnae scream." He had a deerhound on either side of him. One was gray and the other gray and black. Neither moved, their gazes locked on her. One sat and the other was lying down, injured, if she were to guess.

"Who are ye?" she asked, deciding it was best to learn what she could before she screamed. Whatever she'd expected, she hadn't thought to be held captive by a lad no more than twelve winters. The animals were beautiful creatures who clearly adored their master. "Are they yer dogs?"

"My name is Eliot, and these are Thor and Freya. If ye try to hurt me, they'll attack, so it's best ye dinnae try."

Lessons from her mother came back to her, and she had to inquire. "What is wrong with the dog lying down?" The hound was in pain; its eyes darted around the chamber as if expecting something to attack at any moment.

"Freya?" He leaned over to pet the dog's head. "She hurt her paw."

"Why are ye here?"

The boy certainly hadn't brought her here,

so what exactly was his circumstance? Was he a prisoner as well? If the boy trusted her, perhaps he would untie her legs and arms and give her some clue of her situation. He was very thin, with long hair that looked like it hadn't been washed in a moon or more, and his clothing was threadbare. Loki would take him home in an instant, another of the waifs and foundlings who found their way into the Ramsay and Grant clans.

The lad's voice came out uncertainly, almost apologetic. "He said if I watched over ye, he'd feed me and the dogs. Please dinnae be angry. We are verra hungry. Freya is the best hunter, but she canno' hunt because of her paw."

"Where are yer parents, Eliot?"

"I dinnae have any. I lived in a home for orphans, but they were so mean that I ran away. They beat us, and I'd rather risk starvation." The boy rubbed the underside of his arm. A spot where he'd been hurt?

"How long ago did ye run away?" A vision of Loki Grant, Kenzie, Nari, Thorn, and so many others popped into her head. The Ramsays had adopted many orphans, too. Aunt Maggie, Aunt Molly, Simone, Beatris. The list of orphans she knew was long.

"Five or six moons, I think."

The boy looked as though there was little on his bones but skin. No wonder he agreed to do what the bastard who kidnapped her wanted. This poor lad was willing to do anything to put food in his belly.

And to feed his dogs.

Her heart melted. "Where did ye find the dogs?"

"In the woods. I slept in the forest one night last autumn, and I woke up to find them next to me. I had a bit of bread and cheese, and I shared it with them. They follow me everywhere now."

"And how long are ye to watch me?"

"Until the man comes on the morrow. The man who brought ye said I had to stay with ye until then. That he would lock the door from the outside so ye could not get out, and when the man unlocked the door, we could go. He'll send me to the cook and she'll feed me."

"Do I have a few hours to sleep yet?"

"Aye. We do. I'd like to sleep closer to the fire if ye promise no' to attack me." He stared up at the ceiling, waiting for her answer, his hands fiddling with his worn tunic.

She nearly shed tears over the lad's question. "Ye have my word I'll no' attack ye."

He moved closer to the hearth, near enough to absorb some of the warmth from the embers but far enough away that she couldn't reach him.

"Lad, I have an offer for ye."

"Go ahead."

Now that he was closer, she could see the sadness in his eyes, the pale skin, and the dark circles under his eyes. He was so thin that his tunic nearly fell off his shoulders. "If ye untie me, I promise no' to touch ye and I'll help yer pet. Ye see, my mother helps animals that have been hurt, all kinds, and she taught me how to care for them too. I think I could examine yer pet's paw and see what is wrong. And I'll also promise ye this. If I manage to get away to my clan, ye may come with me and join our clan. Ye'll never go hungry again."

His eyes lit up for a moment, but then he became pensive again, staring into the hearth. "What about Thor and Freya? Could they come, too." His small hand reached down to rub the neck of Freya.

Glad to see he was smart enough to consider her offer, she pushed herself to a sitting position. "We would welcome yer pets. In fact, I'm from Clan Ramsay and our chieftain has many deerhounds. He trains them."

"He does?" His hand reached for Thor who moved over to get his ears rubbed, his tongue hanging out.

"Aye. We would love to have ye join our clan. Ye could help in the stables with the dogs and the horses, and ye could sleep there and eat in the great hall."

"Even with the famine, ye have food?"

"We do. Lots of meat. Not as much bread as usual, but our cook knows how to make a great pottage."

Eliot dropped his head, considering her proposal, then reached inside his tunic and pulled out a small dagger, leaning over to cut her bindings. His hands shook, another testament to how hungry he was.

Thea thanked him after he freed her from her bindings, rubbing her wrists where the rope had made her skin raw. She held her hand out to the male dog first. "Greetings to ye, Thor. I promise no' to hurt ye."

He sniffed her hand, then her feet before stepping closer. "I wish I had some food for ye, but I dinnae. But I promise to find ye some." She rose from the cot and stretched, assessing any injuries of her own—only sore muscles and a collection of bruises—before she moved over to the injured dog.

"Greetings to ye, Freya."

The dog growled a wee bit, as did Thor, but she reached for Thor and rubbed his neck to calm him. "I'll no' hurt her. I'm going to help if I can."

Thea sat down next to the injured dog and whispered kind words, rubbing Thor while she reached for Freya, holding her hand out to allow the dog to take in her scent, keeping her fingers inside her fist in case she snapped. Injured animals were always unreliable. Even the kindest could bite from fear or pain.

But she couldn't bear to see the animal hurting. Eliot came over and petted Freya, giving her the comfort she needed with a stranger touching her. Thea took her time, moving her way slowly to the injured front paw, wondering how she could get the dog to lift her paw for her.

"Will she bite ye if ye touch her paw, Eliot?"

"Nay, she'll let me. I've looked at it, but I dinnae know why it's sore."

Thea glanced around the chamber, pleased to see a few candles on a nearby chest. "I'm going to bring that tallow over so I can look closer if ye will hold the paw for me. Mayhap I can fix it."

"Do ye think ye can?"

The hope in his eyes tugged on her heartstrings. She had to help this lad when she got away. "I'll do my best, but ye might have to hold her muzzle so she won't bite me. I'll look first and let ye know if ye have to hold her."

Thea lit one of the candles in the embers before moving over to the dog, setting it close by.

"Shall I hold her paw now?"

"Aye, gingerly. Be careful no' to cause Freya too much pain."

"I will."

Eliot did just as she asked, and she let Freya sniff her before she leaned closer to the animal. Sure enough, deep in the middle of her paw sat a big splinter of wood well-hidden between her pads that she'd picked up from somewhere. The invasive sliver was large enough for her to see, and she was quite sure she could pull it out. But she had to be careful.

Splinters hurt coming out just as much as they did going in, and Eliot was not strong enough to hold the dog if she fought.

Thea remembered something she'd often seen her mother do when treating an animal with a small wound like this. She touched the dog in other places close to the splinter, places she knew would not hurt her, allowing the dog to gain some trust, talking to her with soothing words.

"Eliot, when I say so, I wish for ye to hold her jaw closed for a moment while I pull the splinter out. It will hurt her for a moment, but then she will feel much better."

She just hoped she could pull out the splinter in its entirety. Sometimes, it would leave pieces embedded deeper, and they would need to be cut out. She prayed this would not be the case.

Thea moved her hand again to four different places on the animal's body, then did the same with her other hand, hoping to confuse and distract the deerhound.

"Now."

Eliot wrapped his hand around her muzzle and held it tight. Thea held the paw steady and pulled on the splinter, tugging on it enough that the dog whined. "Hold her, Eliot."

And he did.

She gripped the sharp piece of wood at the base and pulled it out, surprised to see how long the splinter was. She held it up for Eliot.

"Look how big it was."

"Oh my!" Eliot took it from her hand and Freya licked her paw for a few moments, then ventured to stand up. "Look, she's walking. Ye fixed her. What is yer name?"

"Thea."

"Ye fixed her, Thea." Eliot leaned over and hugged his pet, then let her go because the dog had gotten to her feet.

Freya came straight to Thea and licked her hand. "Ye are quite welcome, my sweet girl. We need to keep ye in good form so ye can continue to protect yer owner." Then Freya moved over to Thor as if she needed to tell him too.

Eliot gave her a huge smile and said, "We'll go with ye. But…"

"Good. I expect to be rescued soon."

"Truly? But what about the other man who is coming for ye? Do ye know him? How will ye get away?"

"I have friends who will come for me. They'll find a way inside." Of this she was certain. She just prayed they would be here before dawn. "Ye said something before, Eliot. What was it?"

Eliot stared at the floor for a moment, then lifted his head. "Would there be room for another in yer clan?"

"Aye. Who else would like to join?"

He petted his furry friend for a moment before he looked at her again, his hands fiddling with his tunic. "'Tis a lass. She ran away from the orphanage after I did. But I helped her stay hidden and I brought her food. Could she come too?"

Thea's heart nearly broke. "How old is she and what is her name?"

"Her name is Lorna and she is seven summers. She hides in the church down the road."

Thea gasped. The similarities to her own sister were too much for her—even her name was nearly the same. She had to save this lass. No matter what else happened, she vowed to come back for her, bring her to Ramsay land.

"As soon as my rescue comes, we'll go for yer friend. Which way?"

"She's in the chapel south of here. I thought I could bring her some cheese or bread if I could gain a meal here."

"Think no more on it. I will see she is saved.

But I have one more question about the man who is coming on the morrow."

"I dinnae know much about him, my lady."

She watched him carefully, hoping he knew this much. "Did they tell ye his name, Eliot?"

"Who?" he asked, petting his contented pet.

"The man who is coming in the morn."

"Och, aye. They did," he said, stopping to think for a moment. "I remember because he sounds like he's mean. He was here before, and I watched them talk about ye. I was behind him and noticed that his shoulder was bleeding."

She froze, a vision of the man in the forest as he jumped onto his horse, cursing her out. "His right shoulder?"

"Aye. He's going to take ye away, then sell ye to someone. But I canno' allow him to do that to the person who fixed Freya. Ye are verra nice. I hope ye are rescued."

She took two steps closer to Eliot and whispered, "Think, Eliot. This is important. What is his name? The man with the injured shoulder."

He scowled, then his face lit up. "Fulke. His name is Fulke."

CHAPTER FOURTEEN

WILLUM PACED AT the base of the hill behind the dilapidated castle outside Edinburgh while Dyna and Maitland discussed their plan. Once they met up with Maitland's group, they'd found the castle that had appeared in Dyna's dream without any trouble, Dyna leading them through the winding streets of the outer village and into the edge of the sprawling city. But now that he recalled the words Dyna had used to describe Thea's location—cellar—his stomach reacted.

He could feel the grip of something squeezing his insides at the thought of going inside this crumbling stone wreck of a building.

That old, unwavering something told him to run. To refuse. It was too small. Too dangerous. What if she was truly in the cellars, the one place he dreaded more than any other? He'd passed out in cellars before. This overwhelming feeling of not being able to breathe properly overpowering his clear thinking.

He had to be strong for this lass he was losing

his heart to because he couldn't bear the thought of not having her in his life.

Fortunately, Dyna and Maitland were so busy discussing their plan that they were ignoring him. They didn't seem to notice his pacing, his fright, his need to run into the forest and never return. But he couldn't ignore it. He couldn't deny the sense of something closing in on him, like an iron cuff wrapping around his throat, restricting his ability to breathe. He forced himself to focus on what was most important.

Thea needed rescuing. Thea, the woman who held his heart more tightly than any fear ever could. He had fallen for her and fallen hard. His mother would say fallen in love, but he had no idea exactly what that meant or how it should feel.

He had the incredible need to find Thea then choke the breath out of the bastard who'd dared to touch her. What exactly that meant, he didn't know. Was it love? He had no idea; he only knew he'd never felt this way before.

"Are ye sure ye recall this structure well enough?" Maitland asked Dyna.

"I saw the entire structure in my vision. I stood in the front, then peeked in the window. This is it, I tell ye. She is somewhere inside here, and I believe in the cellar. It was dark and musty smelling, but I tell ye she is in that castle. We'll find her."

"And ye still have that visual strong in yer mind?"

"Aye. I saw her in a small chamber with a hearth and two deerhounds."

Willum remembered her words from the time she experienced the vision. He'd never seen anyone have visions like that. When he'd had the sense at his cottage about Thea being hurt, it had been more of an inkling. He'd had no true vision of her, just the compelling need to find her. He'd been correct, but he had no inkling now.

He wasn't sure if that meant anything, but since Dyna had the reputation of being a seer, rarely were her visions ever questioned.

Maitland scratched his head. "I know ye said so, but did ye see no one inside beside dogs?"

"Possibly a lad is with her."

Maitland arched a brow at her, shaking his head. "That makes no sense at all, Dyna. Why would a lad be with her? She'd overpower him in a moment."

"Not if she's bound." Dyna lost her patience because her next word came out in a near roar. "Maitland!" she said, grabbing his arm with a jerk, as good as any slap Willum had ever seen. "The lad doesnae matter. We need to get inside."

Maitland pulled his arm back with a deep sigh. "I'll trust yer vision. The castle appears deserted at present. I will wait down the path for ye and watch for anyone approaching. Ye and Willum go in to find her. Alaric, Eli, and the others are in front of the castle, and will raise the alarm if they see any activity. If ye dinnae see us in front, we'll be down the path patrolling."

"Aye. I told them if they notice any guards

gathering anywhere nearby, they are to let ye know. The castle looks as if it's deserted, but ye never know until ye step inside. If we come running out and yelling for help, that'll be a sure sign we were wrong."

Maitland gave a grim chuckle. "'Tis a fair plan. I trust ye and Willum to find her." He turned around, looking for Willum. "What's wrong?"

"Naught," Willum replied, wiping the sweat from his brow. "I'll be fine. But I dinnae like standing about and thinking on a plan. I prefer to act on it."

Dyna said, "Then we'll go. The postern gate in the castle wall was hanging off its hinges. We can get in that way, and then into the castle proper. Then we'll start searching."

Willum nodded, pulling on his tight collar.

"Willum, ye go into the cellars, and I'll search the second floor. She'll no' be on the first floor—it's too easy to escape from the ground level. And if ye find her, dinnae worry about the lad. She's befriended him already."

Shite. She'd given him the cellars. This would mean he'd have to pull courage from deep within and ignore all the ramblings in his head about being closed inside.

He would do it for Thea.

They started up the hill. It was more than halfway through the night so he hoped to get inside without awakening anyone in the area.

The two did their best to go quietly. The closer they came to the castle, the more deserted it looked. There were no sounds, no light inside at all, no scent of smoke from the kitchen hearth. Once at the door, he reached for it, opened it slowly, and Dyna peeked inside.

Absolute silence and deep darkness greeted them. She stepped inside and motioned for him to follow her. They stood on the landing of a staircase. The stairway to the cellar was a few steps in front of them, and the stairs up climbed away to their left. She pointed for him to go down while she gestured that she would go up. It would be ungentlemanly to suggest she take the cellars, the more dangerous area to search, even without his claustrophobia. So he nodded in agreement.

"Meet me here when ye have finished yer search," she whispered.

He nodded, then waited for her to reach the top of the steps before descending. He gulped three times, fear of the cellar crawling across his whole body now, but he had to move.

He would go one step at a time. That much he could commit to. His father had taught him to do so once when he'd frozen inside a small castle. There was something about the stone, the coldness of the floor, that made castles different for him. In a cottage, you were not restricted much. If he wished, he could climb out any window of a hut or cottage, or even a manor house, he supposed.

Not here. There were no windows in a cellar. Just. Walls.

He reached the bottom step and was surprised to see no door between the staircase and the passageway. Some places had passages, others didn't, instead opening to a wide space in the cellar, items stored haphazardly.

This was different. The passageway was the narrowest he'd ever seen. He thought his shoulders might brush either side of it.

He stepped inside, but then stepped back immediately. No torches lit, no light to assist in his search at all. He thought of his sire's favorite saying—darker than the inside of a birthing mare. That expression made absolute sense to him now. How could he possibly see where Thea would be?

Peering down the passage, he counted four doors, and the more he waited, the more convinced he was that he saw a bit of light coming from the crack beneath the farthest door.

All he had to do was hurry down the passage, listen outside the door, then open it. If Thea was there, all she'd been forced to endure would be over. If not, he would check the other rooms and then head back up the stairs.

There. He'd made a plan. He stood against the cold wall, his hands now behind him still touching the wall, the fear of letting go too powerful. His heart beat so fast that he swore he was lightheaded just from that alone.

Or was it the fear of what he might find? What if she were dead?

Or what if Thea wasn't here at all? What if Dyna was wrong?

Then he could take his leave.

He promised himself that as soon as he counted

to ten, he would step back into the passage. He could do it. He mopped the sweat from his brow. He couldn't allow that to mar his vision. He took a deep breath and stepped into the passage only to freeze again.

Footsteps came down the steps toward him. He nearly darted, but then he saw her.

Dyna.

"Ye have checked everything?" She gave him an odd look. "What's wrong, Willum?"

"I canno' move." His voice came out in a pitiful whisper, although it embarrassed him so much that if he were any younger, he'd cry.

"I'll go," Dyna whispered, patting his arm. "Ye stay here. There is no one abovestairs. The place is deserted." She headed down the passageway, and the dead silence was ripped apart by the sound of a hound barking.

That changed everything.

He followed Dyna, the sudden worry about Thea's well-being overpowering his fears. She stopped in front of the door where the barking had come from. The dog had gone silent, but they could hear a lad's voice.

"Hush, Thor."

Dyna reached for the handle, but then she pointed. The door was padlocked from the outside. This must be where Thea was being held.

He spun around, looking for any sign of a key on the wall, finally finding it near the ceiling. Dyna would have had trouble reaching it.

"Here, try this." His hands shook enough that he'd rather Dyna try the key in the lock. She'd probably be much quicker at it than his trembling hands would be.

He held his breath as she fussed with the lock. When she finally got it off, she opened the door. And had to duck to keep from being hit in the head with a log.

Thea stood not far away, two dogs guarding her.

A lad stood in front of her, a length of firewood in his hands, raised and ready to swing again.

CHAPTER FIFTEEN

"ELIOT, NAY! 'TIS my friend." Thea called. Eliot kept his weapon up, despite her words. "Someone else is behind her, my lady."

Dyna stepped into the room, and then Thea could see the "someone else."

"Willum!" She launched herself at Willum as soon as he came through the door. She'd never been so pleased to see anyone.

Dyna laughed, then said, "Come, Thea. We have to go." She gave Thea's elbow a subtle squeeze, pulling her away from Willum. Much as she wanted to stay in Willum's arms forever, she knew they had to get out of there.

Fulke could be on his way.

"Aye. I'll tell all once we are away from here." Her hand still gripped Willum's. She didn't wish to let go. Not yet. She turned to her new friend. "This is Eliot, and he's coming with us. He's a good lad and an orphan."

Willum took one look at the lad and handed him a piece of cheese he had tucked into his tunic. "Ye need this more than I do, lad. Are those yer dogs?"

Eliot nodded, already chewing on the cheese. "Many thanks to ye for the cheese, but please let's go. May I bring Thor and Freya?"

"Aye. Hurry," Dyna said, her dagger in her hand as she headed down the passageway. There were still no sounds in the castle, but even so, they raced up the staircase, eager to be gone.

Freya stopped at the base of the steps, her paw held up gingerly.

"Her paw. She'll never make it," Eliot said. Thea could hear the threatening tears in his voice.

"She'll make it, Eliot," Thea said. "The splinter is gone."

"I'll no' take a chance." Willum returned to the bottom of the stairs and lifted the deerhound into his arms. "Go. I have her. She can ride with me when we get to the horses."

"Aye," Dyna said. "We leave none behind, even hounds. Eliot will ride with me, and Freya with Willum. We have Blossom with us, Thea. Can ye ride?"

"I think so."

"Then I'll let Freya ride with Willum," she said, gesturing for everyone to go ahead of her toward the broken fence gate in the back. "Go. The horses are tethered in the forest a short distance behind the fence."

Thea followed Dyna, making sure Eliot was able to keep up. Once they were outside, she had a clearer view of how gaunt the poor lad was. She made a mental note to feed him slowly. He'd probably try to eat everything but wouldn't be able to handle it. That also made her wonder how hungry the poor dogs would be.

Eliot probably fed the dogs before himself.

Once they made it through the broken gate, Dyna pointed and said, "That way. I'll keep guard while ye head to the horses. Thor is right behind ye, Eliot, so keep going. Willum has Freya. Thea, do ye think ye can handle it?"

"Aye, I am a wee bit sore, but that willnae stop me. Just get me away from here. I forgot to tell ye that Eliot said the man coming to collect me was named Fulke. I'm guessing 'tis the same man." She looked to Dyna and Willum to see their reactions to this new information.

Willum muttered something she couldn't hear, then said, "There is probably only one man named Fulke who is that evil."

They reached the horses, mounted, and rushed out, Thor following. The group made their way around to the front of the castle, Dyna glancing around. "Maitland is here somewhere so keep going. If we dinnae see him, he'll catch up."

They'd nearly made it out of the area when a man came out of the front of castle, rubbing his eyes as if he'd been awakened. "Come back, ye wee bastard!"

That didn't frighten them as much as the man coming on horseback from the other direction.

Thea swore it was Fulke Slater. She reached for her bow, but worried because she could feel the slight tremor in her hand.

"Nay, I see what ye are about, but dinnae grab

that bow, Thea," Dyna said, turning in her saddle to retrieve her bow. She stood in the stirrups without stopping her horse. Her first two arrows missed.

The third one struck him in his leg. His horse turned aside, bolting in fear.

"Ye bitch! I'll come for ye, I promise!"

It was definitely Fulke. Thea recognized the maliciousness in his voice.

Eliot's voice came out in a panicked shout. "Is he going to catch us? He'll beat me."

Fulke, now well off the path, managed to stop his horse. Thea could just see him through the trees as he yanked the arrow out of his leg.

Willum called over to Eliot. "Ye needn't worry, lad. His horse canno' catch up with our mounts. These are warhorses and his is on its last legs."

Eliot whimpered, hugging Dyna's back as she urged their mount faster.

"Who is the lad, Thea?" Willum asked.

"Someone they hired to keep watch over me in exchange for a meal. He and his dogs are starving."

A few moments later they met up with Maitland and the rest of the group.

Maitland waved for them to slow down. They could talk while the horses kept up a steady jog. "We're heading back to the inn our group stayed in the first night. I dinnae trust the area ye were attacked in. But we need to talk and make our plans. Nice shot, Dyna. We were just about to come to yer aid when ye nailed him."

"Hell, I missed the first two," Dyna said. Thea

guessed she would have liked to curse more vehemently but didn't because of the boy.

"Ye only needed one. Thea, ye are hale?" Maitland moved his horse to ride abreast of them.

"Aye. Tired and a wee bit sore from riding a horse on my belly, but mostly hale."

Willum reached for her wrist, pulling her tunic sleeve back to reveal the raw spots on her wrist. "Ye were bound?"

"Aye, but Eliot freed me." She shared the lad's story with the men. "I promised to bring him to Ramsay land. We have to help him, Maitland."

Maitland nodded. "He'll be welcome in many places. Ye know that. 'Tis what we do. Menzies, Grants, Ramsays, Camerons. We welcome all."

Thea teared up. She knew exactly what he meant. Their clan and their allies would make Eliot feel welcome and comfortable. She glanced over her shoulder, pleased to see that Thor was still behind them, panting, but he was there.

Then she recalled something else. "Wait! I have one more thing I must do." The memory of Lorna, Eliot's friend, popped into her mind. They had to go back. The chapel where the girl was living, according to Eliot, was in the opposite direction.

"What is it?" Willum asked.

"I'll tell ye on the way, but we must go back south, past the place where I was held. A chapel. We have to find the chapel."

"Ye willnae go back there, Thea," Maitland commanded. "Dinnae take her, Willum."

Eliot began to sniffle, and they all turned to

look at him, but he said nothing despite the tears running down his face. The boy had been through too much.

"His friend. I must go for his friend. Just follow me. I know where she is."

Willum turned his horse around while Dyna argued.

"Thea, ye are no' thinking clearly. Fulke is looking for us. Ye are giving him what he wants." Dyna guided her own horse to block them from going any farther.

Thea gave her head an angry shake. "I dinnae care about Fulke Slater. There is a wee lass of seven summers who was abused in an orphanage. She ran away and stays hidden inside a church. The only one who cares for her is Eliot. I was wrong about the fawn, but no' this. She is a child, not an animal. What if he doesnae return to feed her? What will happen to that lass?"

Dyna groaned. "Hellfire. Lead the way. Eliot, ye will stay back with Maitland." She moved over close to him and handed the lad over.

Thea and Willum trotted south, Thea telling him all that Eliot had said about the lass. Fortunately, they did not run into Fulke again. Once at the small church, Thea dismounted, but Dyna shouted a protest.

"Ye'll no' go alone, Thea!"

Thea stopped, her weakness nearly buckling her knees. Dyna hopped down from her mount. "Willum, watch the horses."

"'Tis just a chapel, Dyna. The minister or priest probably lives at another church and only travels here once a sennight or so." The building was small and looked deserted, though the tall spire commanded the respect it deserved. Thea could feel the beat of her heart and prayed they could find the girl. She knew what everyone would think—that this lass meant something different to her. But it wasn't that. The girl deserved a good life. They would find a place for her on Ramsay land just as they had Simone and Beatris and so many others.

"Where is she?" Dyna asked.

"Eliot said she'll be hiding under the bottom section of stairs."

"What does she look like?"

Thea thought for a moment, then replied, "I dinnae know. He never said. Her name is Lorna."

"Lorna? Do ye jest?"

Thea knew what Dyna meant, but she said only, "'Tis what Eliot said."

They stepped inside and waited for their eyes to adjust. The silence was overwhelming.

When they reached the bottom of the staircase that led to the cellar, Thea moved Dyna aside and stepped behind the staircase. There sat a lass with the most beautiful red hair, her eyes wide. Her fear was so palpable that Thea had to speak to ease her tension.

"Lorna, Eliot sent us. We are taking him and his two dogs to our clan to live, and he asked us to come for ye, too."

A tear rolled down her cheek, and her hands fisted in her lap as she sat on the cold stone floor. Her garments were old and frayed.

"What are the names of his dogs, if ye please?" she asked.

Thea held her smile back. The girl wasn't a fool.

"Aye, she's wise enough to test us," Dyna said.

"My name is Thea Douglas and this is Dyna. We are taking Eliot to live on Ramsay land with us along with his two dogs, Freya and Thor."

Thea touched the girl's forearm and said, "We promise not to hurt ye, Lorna. Ye can work in our kitchens, and we promise to find ye a warm bed inside. We'll feed and clothe ye, but most of all, protect ye against any cruel people who run places for orphans. The Ramsays have adopted many orphans over the years."

The lass wiped the tears from her cheeks and nodded, appearing pleased. She whispered, "I'll come with ye." But she didn't move.

"What's wrong?" Thea asked.

"I canno' move, and I have no mantle to wear."

Dyna said, "I'll help ye get up, and we have extra plaids on our horses. I'll find ye a nice large man to ride with to keep ye warm and safe."

She shook her head so furiously that Thea had a good idea what had happened at the orphanage to make her run away. "Nay, ye can ride with Dyna. Will that suit ye?"

The lass nodded and reached for Dyna who helped her to stand.

Lorna had a new home.

They made it to the inn just after the sun came up. But it seemed she was to have no rest.

Kyle and his son Kyler came out of the inn as they rode in, four Ramsay guards close at their heels.

"Oh no, Willum. I have a bad feeling." Thea held her breath, waiting for what she was sure would be bad news.

Willum rubbed her arm lightly and pulled his horse up close enough to Kyle so they could converse.

"My apologies, Thea. But we are here to fetch ye. Yer sire is verra sick, and yer mother requests yer return."

Dyna looked at Maitland. "Then we all return. We gained a lad, a lass, and two dogs, one with an injured paw. We can decide what to do next on Ramsay land."

"I'll take the other dog," Kyler said. "He'll not keep up with us. I know how fast we'll be riding." Kyle jumped down to get the dog, lifting him onto Kyler's horse.

Thea knew the poor animal wouldn't be comfortable, but they had no choice. Based on the exhaustion in the dog's eyes, Thea thought Thor would accept it.

Eliot looked at Kyle with a wee bit of fear. "My lord, will ye take me and my friend to yer clan? I promise to work hard for food, and I can work for Lorna too. I can work in the stables if ye promise no' to beat me."

"I'm no' the chieftain, but his second in command, lad. My name is Kyle." He held out a hunk of dried meat for Thor now balanced in front of Kyler. "Clan Ramsay welcomes ye, yer friend, and yer dogs, lad, and there'll be no beatings."

Dyna said, "Pass another piece of that meat over here, Kyle. I already gave Lorna something to eat, but we need more. The lad is starving too, and we didnae have much left to give him."

Eliot took the proffered meat with a smile, staring at it and sniffing it before he took a bite.

Thea's tears couldn't be stopped. She glanced over at Willum and smiled as she watched her clanmates take care of two dogs, a lass, and a lad, who she'd already become quite fond of. Once they were settled, the group departed.

Thea said several prayers as they rode into the brightening day. She couldn't lose her father, not after everything else that had happened in her life.

CHAPTER SIXTEEN

THEA JUMPED DOWN from her horse practically before Blossom had fully stopped in front of her cottage.

Willum dismounted, as well, but she put a hand on his arm to stop him coming into the cottage. He needed to tend to his own well-being.

"Go ahead with the others, Willum. Have a good meal, take care of yer horse, and I'll see ye when I'm able. Ye need to be in the open air, not inside these four walls. And please help Eliot and Lorna to settle."

She nearly twirled around, but he stopped her, cupping her face with both hands and kissing her, surprising her.

And he was delicious. His mouth warmed hers, angling over hers as he held her tight, sending shivers from the top of her head to her toes. His tongue teased hers until she met him at his game, and they dueled with a sudden carnality that she loved. Her insides heated and tingled and begged for more. But he ended the kiss, then kissed her forehead while he brushed his thumbs across her cheeks. She was barely able to keep herself standing upright.

This man was making her feel things she'd never felt before.

"If ye need anything, just send someone to find me. Ye know I or anyone else will do whatever ye or yer mother needs," Willum said. "I'll tend yer horse before I go. Blossom is as exhausted as ye are."

"Many thanks to ye," she said. "I must go inside." She ran to the cottage and hurried through the door, praying her father would be seated at the table.

He was not. Her heart beat so fast that she forced herself to stop, grabbing a drink of water from the bucket of fresh well water they kept near the door.

Her mother came into the main part of the cottage from the bedchamber. "Oh, my dear Thea! Ye returned quickly. I'm glad ye are here!"

"Mama," she said, still a little breathless. "How is Da? Please tell me he is hale." She could see the exhaustion in her mother's face. Caring for her father, wondering if he would survive, fear of death—all of that strain was visible on her face.

She waved to Lorana as she clung to her mother's skirts, but then returned her attention to her mother. "I must go see him. May I? Is he awake or sleeping? He'll survive, will he no'? Please say aye."

"Take a deep breath, daughter. Ye are nearly frantic. I dinnae wish for ye to see yer da until ye are calm. Ye may upset him." She set her hands on her daughter's shoulders and moved her over to a chair by the table. "Please sit for a moment."

"All right. I do need to catch my breath," she whispered, smiling at Lorana.

"Thea, stop smiling at yer sister." Her mother's tone was as harsh as she'd ever heard it. "We need to talk before ye visit with yer sire. I'll not have ye upsetting him."

Thea frowned, then glared at her mother. "'Tis a rude comment. Why would ye say such a thing? It pleases Lorana when I smile at her. And I have no intention of upsetting Da."

"Ye know why I say it."

"Nay, I dinnae. Please dinnae upset her, Mama. She's right there listening to us."

"Thea Douglas, 'tis time for ye to accept the truth. And I'll no' allow ye to see yer sire until ye say the words." Her mother crossed her arms over her chest, a look that told Thea she would not budge on the issue. "If ye go in to sit with him and ye talk about yer sister as if she is still here, ye will confuse and upset him. Admit the truth or ye canno' see him until he is better."

"What words? To stop smiling at Lorana? Why would ye say that? I dinnae understand." Then she closed her eyes, forcing herself to accept the truth. The harsh truth she'd chosen to ignore, the truth that upset her so much that no one would mention the lass's name in front of her. She'd deceived herself for months about her sister, simply because she was unwilling to let go of her.

"Aye, ye do." Her mother's hands fisted at her hips and she paced a circle around the room then came back to stand in front of Thea. "Say the words, Thea."

Thea's words came out in a shout. "Ah, Mama. I know the truth, I just dinnae wish to acknowledge it! Must I?"

"Ye do, but ye've allowed yer wishes to fog yer mind. I need to hear ye accept it now if ye wish to see yer sire. Lorana is no' there and ye know it." Her mother's words hit her harder than any fist possibly could have.

Thea bolted out of the chair and backed away from her mother. What had gotten into her? "Mama, please. Why are ye doing this?"

"Because she passed on a year ago. 'Twas just after Yule when we all became sick with the winter fever. We survived it, but sweet Lorana did no'. She's buried behind the house. Ye know it to be true."

Thea stepped back until her back hit a wall. She wished to deny it, even though she knew it to be true. Memories forced their way back into her mind. Fleeting memories of a lass who cried, though no tears came out, of a child whose cry was so weak one could barely hear it. She closed her eyes, visions of the worst moments of her life assailing her.

Lorana. Dear Lorana, who didn't deserve pain.

Memories of her own pain while she clung to Lorana's lifeless body. Of her wails rending the air.

"Nay! Mama, I canno'. I love her dearly. I'll not mention it to Papa, but I must see him." She shoved past her mother and rushed into their bedchamber, flinging herself onto the bed, lying next to her dear father.

His eyes were closed, his breathing shallow and restless, but he had to be able to hear her. "Papa, please come back to me. I canno' lose ye and Lorana too. Ye are my rock, always here for me through everything. If ye'll just open yer eyes, I promise to help ye to heal. I'll do whatever it takes. If I must stay back from patrol, I'll do it." She took a hard look at her father's ashen face, so unlike the strong man she adored. "Please, Papa. Tell me ye are better. Ye canno' leave me now."

Tears flooded her cheeks, and she clung to his arm, tucking herself in close to him above the covers. His large body was encased in a thick, warm blanket. She rubbed his arm and kissed his cheek, pleased to feel his warm skin. She had feared he would be cold to the touch or hot with fever. Perhaps if she spoke of the wonderful things they'd had in their lives, he would wish to awaken and reminisce with her. She had to try something to make him wake up.

"Remember when Lorana was born and her face was so red and her wee fingers made such tiny fists? And she would swing them until she got what she wished, usually more milk from Mama."

Her sobbing slowed as she continued to talk to her father, memories pushing the pain in her mind away for the moment. "Remember the first time she called my name?" She chuckled because she could picture the lass so clearly. "First she said

'Dea,' which became 'Sea' and then it was 'Tea' and then…" She choked back another sob. "And when she was two or three, she would giggle so whenever she bathed in the falling water of yer creation, swinging her arms and laughing so hard whenever the warm water would spray her face that she made me laugh too." She could almost feel her sister's presence. Closing her eyes to will more memories back, she relived some of their favorite times together.

"Do ye recall the first time she had one of Mama's fruit tarts? She smashed it all over her face, the berries coloring her clothing and her hands, and she only said one word over and over again—*more*." Her sister had been such a beautiful child, more beautiful than any of her cousins. Her hair had been a rich chestnut brown, just like her favorite horse's mane. And in the sunlight, it would flicker as if there were flecks of gold sprinkled like faerie dust over the fine strands.

"I miss her, Papa. I want her to come back. I think I was just pretending that she was still here, and I pretended so hard I forgot it wasn't real. I know she's gone, but it pains me too much to think on it." How did one bear such pain? How did her mother go on? Her father? Her grandmother? They never talked about Lorana at all, keeping their grief inside. Thea would never forget her sweet sister, but she knew now that her wishful thinking must have only brought the rest of her family pain. "But above all, I need ye to get better. I need ye. 'Tis all that must be said. I promise to help ye heal in any way I can."

She closed her eyes and fell fast asleep, her hand covering her father's.

When she awakened, it was the middle of the night. Her father's breaths seemed a bit more rhythmic and even. Quite a bit stronger, she'd say if she were asked.

"Please dinnae leave me yet, Da." She thought of dear Willum and how he'd supported her along this journey of theirs, all the challenges they'd faced on their patrols, and one particular Englishman. "I need to ask ye so many questions. Like what do I do about Willum? He's a kind man, witty and handsome and good with animals just like Mama. I fear I've fallen in love with him. But I canno' marry him."

Her father let out a deep sigh and whispered, "Why no'? If ye love him, ye should marry him. Has he asked ye yet?"

"Nay." Her answer came out without conscious thought. When she realized her father had spoken, she gasped and pushed herself up onto her elbows arranging herself so she could look into his eyes. "Da? Yer eyes are open? Ye truly are hale?"

"No' hale yet, but better. Now answer my question, daughter. Ye've blubbered all over me, and I deserve an answer. Why can ye no' marry him if he asks ye? Ye said ye love him."

She settled her head in the hollow of her sire's shoulder. "Because what if I become with child and we have a bairn and 'tis a wee lass who looks like Lorana? And then we could lose her to the fever, and I'd never be able to handle it. What would I do?"

"Thea Elizabeth Douglas. Do ye believe in the Lord?"

"Aye."

"Do ye believe in Heaven?"

"Aye, ye know I do."

"Then where do ye think a wee lass of eight summers would go if she passed on? Where do ye think yer sister is right now?"

The tears came fresh again, but she didn't mind. "She's in Heaven."

"And that's where my wee lassie belongs. She was the sweetest child on the face of our Lord's lands, and I believe she is in His hands and happy. She plays with buttercups in the morning and puppies all afternoon. And yer great grandparents and yer grandfather are all there to watch over her. What else could ye believe? And what do ye think she is doing?"

"I dinnae know what she does. She plays with puppies all day? 'Tis no' so bad."

"Nay, she plays with puppies and also watches over ye and yer brother. Who saved ye from that fool? Who gave ye the courage to fight so hard?"

"Lorana?"

"Lorana and ye. I believe she watches over ye, gives ye the strength ye need when it comes time. And she'll do it when ye have a bairn too."

Thea thought hard on his words. She believed in God and Heaven and that her sister was there. Everything in Heaven was supposed to be perfect, so why shouldn't she be happy about her sister sitting with God and Grandpapa? Had she been looking at this all wrong?

"'Tis all right, lass. Ye are dealing with yer pain, and it takes time. But worry no' about her. Worry about yerself. Ye must start to heal, and if ye have a man who loves ye, ye should enjoy yer time with him."

"And if we have a lass, should we call her Lorana, Papa?"

"Nay. Lorana is her own special person. But I know ye wish to honor her, so what think ye about something similar? Like Nora? Or Ana?"

"Nora. I love it." She actually smiled, her heart blossoming with something new and exciting, and with it came something she hadn't experienced in a long time.

Hope.

Hope for a future for her and Willum. Hope for more time to enjoy her father.

And hope that she could do what needed to be done when the time came.

"I love ye, Papa. And now I must go apologize to Mama." She kissed his cheek and she stepped out of the bedchamber, her heart aching from opposite feelings.

Her father was better, but she'd lost Lorana. How would she ever heal from such a loss?

And what had made her deny it for so long?

CHAPTER SEVENTEEN

A T RAMSAY CASTLE, Torrian was awaiting their arrival near the stables, exactly where Willum had hoped to find him.

Anywhere was better than the great hall. Willum was finished with stone cellars and crowds for a while. One by one, their group dismounted and got themselves and the dogs sorted out.

Dyna gingerly lifted Freya from her spot while Eliot jumped down from his horse, though the lad's knees buckled when he landed. He got to his feet and rushed to Freya's side. Thor joined them as soon as Kyle set him down.

"Dogs?" Torrian asked, a wide smile crossing his face. He'd been less than ten summers when he'd taken his first hound, Growley, on as his pet. All the litters of pups he'd produced since then, valued across the Highlands, were descendants of Growley.

Maitland patted his belly and pointed to the keep. "I've got to eat. Dyna and Willum will update ye on what took place. I'll take the others inside and see if Uncle Logan has any information for us."

"He does. Ye'll see. 'Tis no' getting any better in the Borderlands."

Maitland took his leave while Torrian motioned the group inside the stables where it was warmer. "Thea is with her sire?"

"Aye. She had an adventure of her own. Some bastard snatched her up while we were in Edinburgh, and she was held captive. We were able to rescue her quickly, and we found this fine lad locked up with her. His name is Eliot." Dyna told the story of losing Thea in the crowd and how they'd found her again. "How is Donnan?"

"He's the same. Alive, but taken by a fever of some kind. Brenna doesnae know the cause, but she's been to see him on several occasions with different potions. Time will tell. I hope Thea's presence will help him to improve."

Eliot stood in front of the mighty chieftain in awe, his gaze following Torrian everywhere. The head of Clan Ramsay dropped to one knee and whistled to Thor, and Eliot's smile grew when he saw the attention Torrian gave to the dog, rubbing his ears until his tail wagged enthusiastically.

"Are ye the owner of these two hounds, lad? They are a wee bit different breed than mine." His gaze went to Eliot, who paled but nodded his head.

"Aye, my lord. But…not the owner, exactly. Mayhap I belong to them."

Torrian chuckled. "Aye. That's the way of it sometimes."

Willum explained Eliot's role in more detail,

including the splinter Thea had pulled from Freya's paw.

"She fixed her," Eliot said, taking a step back from the tall chieftain once he stood up.

"I would expect that from Thea. Ye and yer dogs look hungry. If ye go into that compartment on the wall near the door, ye will find some bread for yer pets, and there's a large bucket of water nearby. When ye return, I'll find ye some food, lad. A little later, we'll find them some milk."

Eliot nodded and hurried to the end of the stable, his pets chasing him without question. Lorna sat on a pile of straw, staring up at Torrian, waiting to see what would happen next if he were to guess.

"Lorna, I'll take ye to the hall where ye can warm up and get new clothes shortly."

She nodded and smiled, but then turned away to watch Eliot and his dogs.

"Tell me the rest," Torrian said.

"They're both orphans," Willum said. "He ran away from the orphanage because they beat him. He's been living in the forest since then. Said he woke up one day to find the dogs sleeping next to him and they never left. We're no' sure of her situation, but she was hiding in the cellar in a church—under a staircase. Also left an orphanage so Eliot brought her food. Thea told him he could join the clan if he was willing to work. And then she invited Lorna, who was verra happy to get out of the cellars. Said she dinnae like spiders."

"He'll probably be a hard worker. What about her? She looks weak."

"We know little of either of them, only what Eliot told Thea. I dinnae know what would force a lass to hide in the basement of an old chapel with spiders, but I choose no' to think on it." Dyna spoke quietly so as not to be overheard.

Torrian glanced over at Lorna, the lass still smiling. "Brenna will take care of her. Bathe her and wash her hair, plaiting it for her, I'm sure."

"Ye'll have to fatten him up a bit first. He's starving," Dyna said, nodding toward Eliot. "I think ye could knock him over with a feather, he's so thin. And poor wee Lorna is the same."

"We'll take care of both of them. Dinnae worry." Torrian turned his attention back to Willum. "Who took Thea captive?" Torrian's gaze narrowed as he awaited their answer.

Willum had to control his temper. "The lad said the one who stole her away was going to sell her to a man named Fulke."

"The same one who attacked her on our land?" Torrian asked.

"Aye. He arrived at the castle as we left, bearing a wound in one shoulder and cursing like a devil. He recognized her. If I'd been sure Thea was hale, I would have gone after him. Dyna put an arrow in his leg, so mayhap that wound will end him."

"I hope he dies from the fever." Dyna paced restlessly. "I wish I'd made a better shot and killed him outright."

Torrian scratched the scuff of his beard, a sign that he was deep in thought. "Men like that dinnae die easily. Trust me."

Eliot returned, leaving his two pets busy eating as if they hadn't eaten in days.

Torrian turned to give the young boy his full attention, crossing his arms in front. "I was going to hire a lad to work in the stable. I'm wondering if ye would be interested, Eliot. I dinnae know if ye are aware, but the lass ye helped is my beloved niece, so I am verra appreciative of any help or kindness ye gave her. I will repay it, if I am able."

"I didnae know that." His gaze darted from Dyna to Willum and back to Torrian.

"This is Torrian, the Chieftain of Clan Ramsay. Are ye still interested in joining the clan?" Willum asked.

"Aye, I'll work hard and I dinnae eat much. I can sleep outside. My dogs keep me warm."

"How about ye work in the stable and take care of the dogs? Ye can sleep in the stable with them and ye'll have a nice warm blanket. No Ramsay sleeps outdoors unless they want to." Torrian shot Willum a smile. "I have a new litter of pups coming soon. Will ye help me care for them after they are born? While they are young, I keep them in the stall at the end, away from the horses. I need someone special to care for them. Are ye up to it, lad?"

"Aye, my lord." The tears that appeared in Eliot's eyes told them exactly what this would mean for him—a roof over his head, food to eat, and work he loved.

"I'll introduce ye to the dogs and the stable master after ye eat. Willum, take the boy up to the keep and have Brenna give him some clean clothes and find him a nice warm bowl of stew. Then I'll introduce him to everyone."

The lad threw his arms around the man and said, "Many thanks to ye, Chief. I'll no' let ye down."

"I dinnae think ye will." He patted Eliot's shoulder and then turned to Lorna. He knelt down to talk to her. "Lorna, 'tis too cold out here for ye. I have a sister named Lily and she has a houseful of lasses. She could use some help. Do ye know how to sew? Or have ye ever cut vegetables?"

"Aye, my lord. Mama taught me how to sew a bit before she passed on. And I cut vegetables at the orphanage."

"And yer sire? Did he die too?"

"I never knew my sire."

"I think ye would fit well in my sister's home. Why do ye no' go up to the great hall with Dyna. She'll find ye some warm clothes and some soup. I'll send my sister up to meet ye later."

"Many thanks, my lord."

Torrian took his leave and Eliot hugged Lorna. "I think we can be happy here, Lorna. Do ye no' think so?"

Lorna nodded.

"I think ye'll be happy here, Eliot," Dyna said. "There are lots of lads running about who ye can make friends with. And we have an excellent cook. And Lily knows many lassies for Lorna to befriend. Ye'll see."

Willum and Dyna took Eliot and Lorna to the

keep, and once they had them settled with Aunt Brenna, Willum moved over to Maitland.

"Have ye made any plans? Any news for our patrol?"

"Aye, Uncle Logan has heard more from James Douglas. The English forces in the Borderlands near Berwick have started raiding homesteads and crofts, and Douglas has asked for more swords and bows to help protect the Scots there. We leave to support him in two days. Alaric, Eli, Tevis, and Wenna will go along. Whether or not Thea joins us is uncertain. I hope ye will, Willum."

"I will gladly join ye, but until then, I'll be sleeping in the stables with Eliot. I'll help him settle."

Maitland nodded, giving him a knowing smile. He was not staying in the hall any more than he had to.

He would visit Thea on the morrow.

CHAPTER EIGHTEEN

"MAMA," THEA CRIED as soon as she found her mother fussing over Bo in her outbuilding behind their cottage. Her sire had built it for shelter for both the animals and her mother, giving her the warmth and protection of walls, and divided it into two sections. One side had a hearth for the smaller animals, and the larger section did not have a hearth. She helped animals of all sizes so, so he'd built an area with a stone floor and a roof and finished it with thick walls to protect her from the elements. There were a few different enclosures in the larger section to keep sick animals separated along the wall.

As soon as Thea entered, Bo tried to escape her mother's ministrations. Thea rushed across the room, calming him quickly, his cold nose reaching to greet her once she was close. "Mama, forgive me for my sharpness last night. I was wrong. Ye know I love ye dearly, but I was so upset about Da and Lorana. He is awake now, and..." She let out a deep sigh. "And I know Lorana is in Heaven with Grandpapa."

"I am glad this is settled in yer mind now. I miss Lorana too. In fact, I think of her every day, but I must continue to live my life here. I will see my sweet lassie again someday. It took me a while to accept her loss and ye are young. It has taken ye longer."

"My deepest apologies for my harsh words. I dinnae know what came over me. I will accept her passing as truth now," Thea said, not saying the last thought she had in her mind. If she didn't carry the guilt she did over Lorana's passing, she may have been able to accept the truth much sooner. But she couldn't speak those words. Not yet.

"Worry. I've heard rumblings about yer journey from others already, and ye had an interesting patrol. 'Tis what came over ye to jumble yer thoughts. Ye've been traveling on patrol, worrying about whether ye would be attacked and ye were. I recall being off Ramsay land in trying times, and I feared everyone and everything. And after I was attacked by Bearchun, I had even more fears. Those kinds of thoughts keep ye from looking at things the way ye should. Thinking of yer sister with me was probably a comforting thought."

"It was." She didn't know how to tell her mother how jumbled her thoughts had been. "Papa woke up in the middle of the night. We had a nice chat, and I hope that means he will heal."

"I overheard ye talking and that pleases me greatly. 'Tis a good sign that yer sire will heal. I slept in yer bed so I wouldnae bother the two of ye. I will check on him in a moment. But first, tell me ye'll no' be leaving just yet. Ye must heal from this last attack. And…"

Thea could tell her mother was about ask her for something she wouldn't like. "And?"

"And consider not going on the next patrol. I see yer wrists were bound. Where else were ye hurt? I think ye should stay home and rest for a wee bit and join the next one instead."

She shook her head. If the patrol was leaving, and Willum was going along, then she would be with them. She wished to spend more time with Willum, but she also had that driving need that would not leave her until she saw it through. Getting her vengeance on Fulke Slater was even more important now. Even though the evil man had never touched her in their most recent encounter, it was his fault she'd been taken captive.

"We'll see. Tell me about Bo." She looked at the stitches in his fur and the covering her mother had put on them to keep Bo from licking.

"He's tried to remove them four times. Before he became ill, yer sire was trying to put something around Bo's neck so he couldn't reach it. Hasn't managed to make it work yet. Bo's had a bit of fever, but he came through it. I hope he doesnae get worse."

Thea perused her mother's fine needlework. "Ye did a lovely job, Mama. 'Tis nearly healed already."

"Many thanks. Soon enough I'll no' be able

to do such fine tasks. My eyes are failing me. I canno' see up close the way I used to. I'm glad I trained ye."

She thought about the many times her mother had helped her practice stitching animals' wounds. Thea had been surprised to find that helping animals gave her a strange sense of comfort. But could she do it all the time? She wasn't sure.

"I thank ye for saving him, Mama." She gave her mother a swift hug after releasing Bo.

"Have ye heard any more about yer attacker?"

"Aye, he's in Edinburgh. I know no' where for sure. I hope we will look for the bastard." She told her mother about the adventures of their patrol and the the run in with Fulke outside the castle.

Her mother scowled her disappointment at her cursing. "Mama, I'm old enough."

"I know. I canno' fault ye. The man surely deserves no better."

They both heard the approach of a horse, so Thea went to the door and peeked out, pleased to see it was Dyna.

Dyna saw her as she approached the cottage and called out, "How is yer sire?"

"Better. I'll be right out, Dyna." She hadn't had the chance to talk to Dyna about how she might pursue her mission of seeing justice done for women who'd been attacked by men. Perhaps now was a good time.

"Nay, no need to meet her outside. Have Dyna join ye back here out of the elements. I'll go see yer da." Her mother left, and Dyna came in, greeting her mother as they swapped places.

Thea sat next to Bo, giving him a bone to chew on while she chatted. "News for me?"

"Nay. I wished to see how ye and yer father both fared. We'll be leaving again in two days, but ye need no' join us if ye arenae ready."

"I'll be ready. Ye can be sure about that. As long as Fulke Slater is looking for me, I think it best for me to be away from home."

Dyna eyed her curiously, but then sat near Gerland so she could pet the animal.

"Dyna, may I ask ye something?"

"Of course. I'll answer if I'm able."

"I was considering what to do with my life— my purpose, as my sire calls it. Not all women can or will fight back like we can, and it upsets me that no one stands up for them. Do ye think that I could make it my mission to help them? Find a way to stop their abuse? Like the man who tried to accost ye. He'll no' try again after dealing with ye."

Dyna snorted. "I wish it were that simple, lass. That man will find another woman to abuse, one who doesn't carry a dagger tucked inside her boot. 'Tis most common. Many men—no Ramsays, of course, that I know of—abuse their wives all the time. But just because it's common doesn't mean it's easy to fight. To spend all yer time dedicated to such an endeavor would be admirable, but I fear 'twill no' keep ye busy."

Thea frowned, surprised by Dyna's answer. "But why no'?"

"Because most husbands do their best to keep

it hidden. Some are proud of the way they treat their wives; they think 'tis their right. But most are embarrassed so they keep it quiet. Often they tell their wives to keep their mouths closed. They surely dinnae want the woman's family to know how he treats her. Torrian will send a man out of the clan if he catches them abusing their wives, but he is a rare chieftain. And the women feel shamed, whether it was her husband who hurt her or a stranger, like that man who made a grab for me."

"So ye havenae come to another woman's aid often?"

"Nay. I'm sorry to give ye that news, but ye'll no' uncover many. 'Tis why the band of cousins struggled so. The men kept their despicable work hidden."

Thea chewed on this information, feeling lost again.

"Why do ye no' think yer mother's skills are admirable? I thought ye enjoyed working with animals." Dyna scratched Gerland behind his ears.

"I do, but…she does most of it. She doesnae need me."

"When yer mother passes, Clan Ramsay will have no healer for the animals. Ye know her work is invaluable to the clan. Who will take her place?"

Thea covered her ears at the awful thought. After losing her sister, watching her brother fall off his horse, and fearing her father would pass too, she was not ready to think on anyone else dying in her family. "Please, dinnae say such a thing. I'll no' lose my mother yet. I couldnae handle it."

"I expect Bethia will be with us for a long time. And I hope yer sire will be too. I dinnae think ye need to decide this moment. I think working on patrol to protect Scotland is an admirable task. Ye can focus on that." Dyna stood, brushing some of the dog hairs from her clothing. "'Tis enough for now."

"I will, but I do have one more important purpose at present."

"What?"

"Vengeance." Her gaze locked on Dyna's to gauge her reaction. To her surprise, Dyna did not look happy. "Dyna, he's tried to attack me twice. Or attacked me once, then hoped to sell me."

"I feared ye would say that. Please promise ye willnae try to take that vengeance on yer own when there are so many English around. Did ye know that Logan heard the men in Berwick Castle are so hungry that they have begun to eat their horses?"

Thea gasped. "What a horrible thought! That makes me ill."

"Edward sends them no rations because of the famine. They may end up dying from starvation. Or worse, cannibalism."

She couldn't comprehend that thought, but she didn't believe Fulke Slater was working for King Edward. He was stealing for his own benefit, and he would not be giving up anytime soon. And he'd promised to come for her. She'd be ready when he did.

Or she'd be going after him. He thought her a helpless female.

She'd prove him wrong.

CHAPTER NINETEEN

WILLUM CHECKED ON Eliot, who was settled and happy in the stables. The lad patted his belly for emphasis.

"'Tis full now?" Willum asked.

"Aye, three times a day 'tis full. I used to be pleased if I could find one meal a day. And my dogs are fed too. I love it here and so does Lorna. The air is fresh here, it does no' smell like Edinburgh. Many thanks to ye and Thea. Where is she? When might I see her?"

Willum chuckled. He had to agree with the lad. The city always smelled like raw sewage to him too, though it was always a bit better near the castle. "I'm going to visit her now. If she's hale, I'll bring her to see ye."

Willum smiled, pleased that Eliot was now happy and had a home. Not the kind with parents, but a place where he belonged. The guards would see that he was taken care of, just as they did all the stable lads.

But he was worried about Thea, and he could not put his visit off any longer. Aye, it would be good to see if her sire was faring better, but it was more important to check on her.

After all, she'd been held captive, which had to have left her unsettled. If he could help her get through this threat of Fulke Slater plotting to attack her, he would do whatever he could.

He also had a fear that she would go after the villain herself. His other goal today was to convince her not to and leave it to him to give the cruel bastard his just due.

As he approached the cottage, he was surprised to see Dyna leaving. She slowed her horse when they met.

"All is well? Her sire is better?" he asked Dyna.

"Aye. He is still sickly, but improving. Talk with Thea. I suggested she stay back for this patrol, but she claims to be ready. I fear she is acting on the single thought of finding Fulke Slater. 'Tis no' good to have someone on patrol focused on a different purpose than the rest of the group."

"I understand what ye mean. At least she'd be focusing on someone whose intent is to harm or steal from us. He's English. Does that no' fit with our general purpose?" Willum had to admit that patrolling without Thea was not appealing to him. If she needed to stay back to heal, he would understand. He just had to pray that if she did stay behind, it was not so she could go after Slater on her own. Perhaps he'd speak with her mother to let her know to keep an extra eye on her.

"Aye, in a way," Dyna said. "But general purpose only. See what ye think of her overall readiness for patrol. We'll talk when ye return to the hall. I dinnae wish to put her at risk for anything."

"I will." He waved to Dyna as she left to head back to the hall. He understood Dyna's concerns. Having someone looking for something different on patrol than the rest of the group was not going to be productive. Focusing on finding one man so exclusively that they let scores get by them would not sit well with any of them.

When he brought his horse to the small stable Donnan had built, he was surprised to see Thea out back with Bo and Gerland, allowing the animals to chase squirrels.

"The dog needs exercise? Is that what propels ye outside on this cold morn, lass?"

She whirled around and her face lit up. He was more than pleased to bear witness to such an event. It made his trip worthwhile.

"Willum, I am so glad to see ye." She stopped as he approached her, taking one last look around to make certain they were alone. Then she wrapped her arms around him for a hug.

That wasn't enough for him, so he tugged her in close and said, "If ye dinnae wish for a kiss, say so now."

She grinned and leaned in closer. "There's naught I would rather do at the moment."

He cupped her face before his lips descended on hers, and he did what he'd wished to do for so long. He kissed her lightly at first, but then his hunger for her overpowered him, and he ravaged her mouth, angling his over hers so he could deepen the kiss and taste all of her. He'd had a brief kiss when he'd dropped her here after patrol, but that only convinced him that he wanted more from this beautiful lass.

Her soft curves melted against his body, and he wanted nothing more than to make her his right at that moment, but he knew it was impossible. She had no idea what power she held over him or that every day, he fell for her a wee bit more.

He pulled away just enough to kiss a trail down her neck and back up again to her ear, his tongue teasing her until she shivered in his arms.

"Thea, ye are so beautiful. The most beautiful lass I've ever seen."

He ended his assault to look into her eyes, taking in her swollen lips and the hooded desire in her gaze. How he wished to see her next to him every night before he closed his eyes and every morn after he awakened. They would make a fine pair, and the need to make her his wife became stronger every time he saw her.

But the reality was that he needed to get ready for patrol. The group would be heading out soon enough. There was no time for a wedding, and he would not propose until Fulke Slater was no longer a threat.

She snuggled up against him. "I wish we had more time alone, Willum. How can we ever get to know each other with a patrol around us at all times?" Her breathing came out in short pants, telling him that she had enjoyed their interlude as much as he had.

"'Tis difficult, but now that I am sure ye have the same feelings, I will make it a priority to find more time alone for us." His playful grin delighted her.

"I would like that," she whispered, blushing.

Gerland came racing back toward them, bumping into Willum as if asking to be petted, so he bent down and gave the animal the attention he sought. Soon enough, the hound pulled away and disappeared, heading back to the woods, probably wanting to check on Bo who was moving about more slowly, busy sniffing everything he could.

"Would ye like to go for a ride, my sweet?" he asked, glancing up at the sky. "The sun is out and ye might enjoy it now that spring is nearly upon us. I promise not to ravish ye again."

"I'll go, but only if ye promise to ravish me again sometime." She giggled when he waggled his brow at her.

"I absolutely will make that promise."

Thea stepped inside to tell her mother they were leaving, telling her where the dogs were, then they headed out to the stable together. Willum lifted her onto her mount. "Dyna told me yer sire is better."

"Aye, he has improved. I slept next to him last eve, and he awakened to speak with me in the middle of the night. I feel so much better. I canno' leave him just yet, though. I need him still. He gives such good advice that I'd be lost without him."

"I'm glad he's improved. I know his sickness will make it difficult for ye to return to patrol. Will ye stay back for a bit?"

"Nay. I'm going after that bastard, Fulke Slater.

Now that we know he bears a grudge against me, I must put an end to this, Willum. Surely ye understand. He'll not give up until he repays me for wounding him." She led her horse toward one of the more popular paths that led off Ramsay land.

He knew they had a long way to go before leaving their land, but he guessed she didn't wish to head toward the castle. He had to agree with her. He'd rather have privacy.

Willum hated to hear her say it, but he believed her words about Fulke were the truth. She'd never settle until the man was found and imprisoned. Or dead. He said the only thing he could to make the situation better. "I pledge to help ye in this endeavor. If we find him, we will follow him until we convince him no' to follow ye again."

"Many thanks to ye, Willum." They stopped their horses on the path where the forest was thick on both sides, the lack of wind and rain making it so quiet that they could hear every rustle and birdcall. "Do ye hear something? Not on the path but in the woods?" She swore she heard voices, but it was in the woods, not on the path.

Thea's head swiveled, an intent look on her face, scanning the area. "I hear voices," she said, motioning for him to be quiet.

He moved his horse closer, the forest endless on two sides. "I hear them too. Male voices. Where do ye think they could be?"

"Uncle Logan used to meet some of his messengers in the woods somewhere near here.

Not far from our line." Nearly everyone knew Logan used to be a spy for the Scottish Crown, so the word didn't really hold true any longer, but he loved to be secretive about many things. "Do ye suppose he meets the men from King Robert out here?"

Willum replied, "I suppose. He always mentions a messenger giving him information, but I never see the men he refers to. Have ye seen them?"

She shook her head, her gaze narrowing as she honed in on the sound. She indicated an area in the trees. "There. I think they're behind this row of trees. Do ye think they are reivers? Do ye recognize any voices?" Thea would recognize any Ramsay guards.

She held her finger up to her lips and moved her horse closer. Then she pointed toward the voices and then her ear, so he moved his horse close to the same spot.

It sounded like Logan Ramsay, and based on Thea's wide-eyed look, he was right.

They both leaned toward the sounds and listened.

"What did ye learn?" Maitland asked. "Anything about the English?"

Logan snorted. "Aye, but not what we hoped to hear."

"What the hell does that mean, Uncle Logan?" Maitland asked. After so many days on patrol with him, Willum had no trouble recognizing his voice.

"Spill all. None of yer games of playing secrets." This woman's voice sounded like Dyna.

Willum whispered, "Should we interrupt them? Let them know we are here?"

"In a moment," she replied, holding her hand up.

"There's a rogue Englishman, originally one of Edward's men from Berwick. Says he's hunting for food, but he's looking for something else."

"Something else or someone else?" Dyna asked. "He had better not come close to Ramsay or Menzie land."

"Word is he's headed this way. He's looking for a Ramsay."

Willum glanced at Thea, her eyes now widened. He had the impulse to come through the trees and let them know they were there, but she held her hand up to stop him. He understood why. His grandfather was infamous for keeping secrets. If this conversation was about Fulke, they wouldn't tell her.

Thea wanted to know. She deserved to know.

Maitland groaned. "Hellfire, say 'tis no' true. Say he is no' coming this far north."

"They say he is nearly here. He's alone, on horseback. Hiding whenever anyone comes near him. A sheriff who found him on the road near Menzie land told him to go back south. But he's ignoring the sheriffs and staying well hidden. Going slowly through the forest, but near the main path to find his way. He doesnae know the area well enough to take the other paths."

"And a sheriff sent a messenger? Why are we just now hearing about him, if he's been moving so slowly and is nearly here?" Maitland asked.

"Because the sheriff who's been tracking him finally discovered his name," Logan said.

"Who the hell is it?" Maitland demanded.

"Fulke Slater."

CHAPTER TWENTY

T HEA DID HER best not to react. She did
not want her uncle to know she'd been
eavesdropping. She stared at Willum, and he
reached for her hand.

Dyna's voice came again. "I'm going back. We
should leave on patrol midday tomorrow instead
of two days. We can search for the bastard while
we head south. Do we tell her?"

"I think we should," Maitland said. "Everyone
needs to be on guard. Ye canno' have yer guard
down with that bastard."

Logan grunted. "He's only one man who's wild
from vengeance eating at his soul. They say he
carried two visible wounds. His shoulder and his
leg and he's still bleeding through his trews. No
need to tell her if she's no' going on patrol. He'll
be dead soon. I'll tell Torrian and he can handle
it."

"If she's no' going, then she needs to move to
the keep. We should tell her and her mother. They
should no' be out in that cottage without at least
a couple guards, especially since Donnan is ill and
Drystan is back with the Grants. Slater is familiar

with that area since he met her close to there before." Maitland was more than insistent, his tone impatient. "They canno' stay there alone."

"Since she's probably going with us, I say we tell her," Dyna said. "And make sure her mother is guarded as well. In the meantime, I'm going back in the hall. Too cold out here. I take a hearth when I can. There was no reason to meet way out here, Logan. Enough with yer secrets. Just tell everyone what ye learned."

"Mark my words, Dyna. Sometimes the truth causes people to act without reason. Ye'll see someday. Some things are better kept hidden."

The group broke up, and Thea and Willum locked gazes, both of them waiting for the others to take their leave. The sound of hoofbeats carried to them, so they waited until they were far away before they spoke again.

Thea had mixed feelings over what happened. Guilt over eavesdropping yet upset with her great uncle that he could even consider keeping this information from her both consumed her. She had a right to know the truth.

Thea wasn't sure how she felt about the news, except that this was her chance to kill the bastard Slater. Could she do it? She tried not to think too hard on Uncle Logan's words about vengeance in the man's soul driving him mad and what it might do to her.

"Ye will go on patrol with us?" He squeezed her hand, then lifted it to his lips, kissing each finger separately.

"Aye. I must," Thea replied, shivers coursing

through her. "I will see this through. Besides, I'd rather be traveling with ye than to be here without ye. Being at home, finally admitting that Lorana is gone, 'tis too painful to sit in my cottage. Drystan took his leave; Da is ill. 'Tis too painful. Going on patrol will keep my mind active. And I want to search for the fool, not wait for him to come find me."

"Do ye wish to talk? I'm no' sure I understand all ye just said. What about Lorana? I thought she passed on a while ago?"

It was time to be truthful with Willum about everything. "Do ye have a moment? If so, I'd prefer to have this conversation with ye alone. Could we sit in one of the clearings? 'Tis a warm enough day for a short conversation." Thea trusted Willum more than anyone right now. At least, trusted that he would listen and not judge her too harshly.

"Of course," he replied. "Lead me wherever ye wish."

Willum followed her to a nice area with a large flat boulder in the middle. He had an extra plaid, and he spread it across the boulder to make it warmer for Thea. Another one of the little things that he did that made her fall for him a wee bit more. He was handsome, a fierce warrior, yet so gentle and kind. There was a softness to him that wasn't often seen in men. That part of him reminded her of her sire.

Once she was settled, she folded her hands in her lap and began her story. "When I came home upon learning my father was sick, his illness frightened me back to the truth of my circumstance, no matter how I wished to deny it. And I was aware of it, but didnae care if anyone knew. People would not mention things to me because I would react badly, and now…now I realize how foolish that was of me."

"Foolish? Whatever ye were hiding from, I doubt it was foolish."

He reached for her hands and cocooned them inside his own, warming her. She loved to look at his hands against hers because his skin had darkened from the sun so much more than hers.

"I denied my sister's death." There. She'd said it. She admitted the truth to him and waited for the condescension that would surely come. Except it didn't.

"I could understand that," Willum said.

Surprised by his reply, she considered which way to steer the conversation next. She'd been braced for condemnation, and now she floundered for what to say.

Willum continued. "I say that I understand because I watched my mother do the same with my sister's death. She never wished to mention her name again. My sire wished to make a lasting tribute to Annis, but my mother wanted no part of it. In her own way, it would mean admitting that she died, and maybe she also carried some guilt about my sister's death. Is that yer situation?"

He gazed into her eyes, the back of his fingertips coming up to graze her cheek. It was time to admit the truth. The truth she'd never admitted to her parents.

"When I went to bed that night, Lorana was quite feverish. She didn't wish to be alone—sometimes I think she thought I was Mama instead of me—but she didn't wish to be left alone. We slept in the same bed, as sisters often do. That eve, I agreed to sleep close to her, even though she was so hot that I swear my skin was scorched.

"Many times, I've chastised myself for not making her drink more water, or for no' going to Mama to tell her how hot she was. But Mama had just started recovering from her own fever, and Da was still sickly. Even Drystan was still lying in bed most of the time. I tried to take care of Lorana on my own, but I…"

"Nay, whatever ye say. I dinnae believe it. But go ahead, finish yer sentence."

"I failed. I blame myself for her death. I failed my sister, so the only way I could handle that guilt was to deny she ever died. I convinced myself that Lorana was always behind my mother's skirts." She paused. She'd teared up, and she wanted to maintain control. "I made myself believe that if I left and came back that she would still be here."

"Ye ran away from the truth."

"Aye." She dabbed at her tears with her fingers, brushing them away from her face. "If I wasnae home, it was easier to believe she was still alive."

"So why do ye tell me this?"

"I needed to confess to someone…" She peeked up at him, hoping she wouldn't see any condemnation in his eyes, but then she dropped her gaze to the ground again.

"Confess what?" he asked, his fingertips going to her chin, lifting her gaze back to his. "Ye have naught to confess that I can see."

"But I do. If I had told Mama, Lorana may have lived."

"Nay, lass. It sounds like she was verra ill. I'm not sure even Aunt Jennie could have done anything, if she was no' drinking and her fever burning so fiercely. We lost many to that fever, ye might recall, and I dinnae think ye can change that. It was Lorana's time. And ye were no' the cause of any of it. 'Twas no' yer fault she passed on. 'Twas the fever's."

She leaned forward and fell into his embrace, resting her chin on his shoulder. "I dinnae know why I denied losing her for so long. What is wrong with me?" she cried, wrapping her arms around Willum's waist.

"'Tis naught wrong with ye that I can see."

He pulled back and kissed her forehead lightly. Then his lips trailed a line of kisses across her cheek and down her neck until she squealed. He laughed and kissed her lips this time, a sigh escaping her as he devoured her. His hands traveled down her back and then underneath her until he lifted her onto his lap.

Their kiss ended, and she whispered, "That was a neat trick getting me on yer lap. Ye did it so smoothly."

"Because I wish to be closer to ye, my sweet Thea. If things were different, I would make ye mine, but no' this day. 'Tis no' right. Ye are hurting and I wish to do what I can to banish that from ye."

She hummed contentedly and said, "Then kiss me again. I forget everything when ye touch me, Willum."

He complied, laying her back on the boulder and kissing her with gentle passion. She giggled when his short beard tickled her.

"Like that, do ye?" he asked, and he proceeded to waggle his chin across her cheeks and down her neck.

She squirmed and shrieked, and he mock-growled in reply, until they slid off their boulder with a bump. Willum caught his weight on his arms so he wouldn't land on her. His smile faded.

"I'll tell ye one thing that's yer fault and no others," he said seriously.

Thea's heart thudded hard once, then seemed to stop altogether. "What?" she whispered, not sure she wanted to hear his answer.

"Making me fall for ye, Thea Douglas."

"Oh, Willum!" She shivered, despite his body heat. "I'll be glad to suffer the consequences for that any time."

"Come. I will take ye home. 'Tis getting chilly out and yer mother will wonder where ye are."

"Aye, ye are correct. Many thanks for listening to me, Willum." And she had to admit, it was as if a weight was lifted from her shoulders, the guilt of causing her sister's death. His words were true. It was not her fault. And she would happily take the blame for that other thing.

They mounted their horses and moved back

in silence, happy in each other's company. Once they were close to her cottage, Willum asked, "Ye are sure yer sire is enough better that ye can leave?"

"Aye. I have the rest of today and tonight to be with him before we leave for patrol on the morrow. I'm glad it has been moved up a day. Suits me fine." She glanced over at Willum, her rock in everything now. Somehow she knew he would always be there for her. "My thanks for being by my side." Her voice cracked but she vowed not to shed a tear. She had to be strong.

"Always." He leaned over and gave her a kiss, and it left her wanting more. It was more than a quick peck, his tongue mating with hers briefly.

A kiss she would remember.

He shifted in his saddle when they reached the door of her cottage. "I will see ye on the morrow, and I promise ye, I will help ye find him."

Thea suspected her mother would be watching, so instead of getting another kiss, she hopped off her horse and waved goodbye, leading Blossom to the stable.

They were leaving on the morrow and would search for Fulke Slater, but that wasn't soon enough for her.

She headed for the cottage, a plan forming in her mind.

She knew it was incredibly foolish, but now that she knew Lorana would watch over her, she felt it would be worth the risk. The middle of the next day could be too late. If all went well and she found Slater close by, as she suspected she would, she'd be back before midday. Then the patrol could do their proper work for King Robert.

She wanted nothing more than for the fool to be gone. No more threat of torture or pain. She'd catch him when and where he least expected her.

Apologies to everyone would come later. She wished to speak with her father again, then she would chat with her mother during the evening meal before taking to her bed early. Then she would sneak out after dark, find a warhorse, and go after Fulke Slater.

Before he got to her first.

Eliot woke up to the sound of one of the horses coming out of its stall. Not feeling that he belonged quite yet, he knew he didn't have the authority to confront anyone about a midnight ride. Whoever was taking out a horse could do as they wished. He cleaned the stalls and fed the horses and dogs and was still learning that job. He had no idea who might or might not be permitted to take out a horse.

Still, it could be that the stall door wasn't latched properly and the horse was taking itself out, so he got up and looked.

He was more than surprised to see Thea taking one of the large warhorses, already tacked up, out of the stall at the end of the stable. He stood in the aisle between the stalls and watched her. She stopped and put her finger to her lips when she saw him.

He would do anything Thea asked of him. If not for her, Eliot wouldn't be here. She was the one who told the others she was taking him with her. It was Thea who had promised he could join Clan Ramsay.

He'd never go against her.

She took a small bag of oats, then waved to him, taking her leave. He didn't move at first, because he didn't wish to upset her, but after she left, he treaded quietly to the end of the stable, peering out into the night. Since he was in the stable outside the curtain wall, she could leave Ramsay Castle easily enough, and Ramsay land completely in the space of a short ride.

And he guessed that was exactly what she was doing. He stared out into the moonlit night, no clouds overhead to block the bright celestial object, giving him a view of Thea as she moved to the mounting block and climbed onto the horse, patted his neck, and headed toward the main path off Ramsay land. A dog, the same lanky shape as his own, followed her. It had to be one of her hounds.

Thea was leaving alone. There was only one thing for him to do.

Follow her.

"Come, Thor. We have work to do."

CHAPTER TWENTY-ONE

———⚬⚬⚬———

THEA SET HER horse into a gallop. Everyone would be upset with her. She'd promised many of her friends and family that she would not go after Fulke Slater on her own. But she wouldn't risk his hurting anyone else. This was between her and Fulke. All the fears she'd had before—fear of being alone—didn't matter until Fulke was dead. *He* was the biggest threat to her family right now, so taking care of him would also relieve some of her fear.

She'd brought Gerland with her in case she needed to send him to find Torrian. She certainly would not let him fight—she could not handle his being hurt. Not after almost losing Bo and the upset of the last day's realization about Lorana.

It was a few hours before dawn, so she didn't expect to see many on the road. The main path was wide enough to let the moonlight through to light her way. Now she just had to hunt for the bastard.

They said he was near Menzie land when he'd been found, so she thought about the distance from there to Ramsay land. She guessed that he would be aiming to arrive on Ramsay land in the dark and would probably head straight to the area she'd seen him in before.

Stopping her horse, she closed her eyes to recall the many trips she'd taken and did her best to conjure up the place between Ramsay land and Menzie land where one could get fresh water.

And then she knew. "I have it, Gerland. I know exactly where he's hiding. He could be on Ramsay land in less than an hour from there. Ye'll see I'm right."

More than once she had stopped at a spot where a creek ran near a clearing at the base of a hill. A small overhang—they'd called it a cave when they were wee lads and lassies—could be used as shelter from the elements overnight. The trees grew thickly between the clearing and the path, giving additional protection to anyone inside.

She knew the area well enough that she decided to walk as she drew near, so she would move more quietly than the big warhorse. She tied her horse to a tree branch, then leaned down and whispered to her hound.

"Gerland, stay."

Gerland obeyed, though he might not if a rabbit darted in front of him. She crept closer, hoping to peer through the trees. She heard voices before she saw anyone. They were unrecognizable, but there were two or three different ones.

She waited, vowing to keep quiet until she knew who was in the clearing.

"Where is she?" one man shouted.

Freezing in place, Thea held her breath as she

waited for a response. She didn't know Fulke's voice that well, but it definitely could have been the bastard.

The next voice she recognized.

She was so sure that she ran back—still trying to be as quiet as possible—to where her horse was tied up, leaned over to Gerland, and commanded, "Torrian, Gerland. Find Torrian and bring him here."

All the dogs knew who Torrian was since he was the breeder of the pack, so she was confident he would find the chieftain and lead him here. And if she wasn't here when they returned, Gerland would follow her scent. Even sighthounds knew how to track.

She wouldn't risk anything happening to the other person in that clearing.

It was Eliot, and Fulke had him.

Willum woke up just as the eastern sky began to lighten. The air was full of barking and yelling coming from the keep and courtyard. Something had happened.

Thea. She'd gone after Fulke. He'd stake his life on it.

He'd suspected she'd leave sometime today to go after him, and he had been surprised when she said she would wait and join the patrol. But he certainly hadn't expected her to sneak away in the middle of the night.

She'd apparently changed her mind about going with the larger group.

He swore, angry with himself for not expecting it. He should have spent the night keeping watch on her cottage. It made no difference to him if he slept under a tree outside Ramsay Castle or Thea's home. He hurried toward the stable, wanting to find out the situation as soon as possible.

He threaded his way through the small gathering of Ramsay guards just inside the gate, looking for someone to ask. Maitland was off to the side speaking with Dyna so he moved over to see what they knew.

"What has happened, Maitland?" Willum asked.

"Thea is missing. We are guessing she went after Fulke."

"She went on her own?" Willum tried not to give any hint that he and Thea had overheard the conversation with Logan the previous afternoon. "The stubborn woman."

"We're unsure of that. Eliot is also missing, along with two dogs—Thor and Gerland— and two horses. There are other possibilities. Mayhap Fulke grabbed Eliot and used him as bait, knowing Thea would do whatever he asked if it meant protecting Eliot. Maybe the two being missing are no' connected at all." Maitland looked to Dyna. "Any ideas? Have ye seen anything in yer dreams?"

Dyna closed her eyes and looked as if she were listening for something no one else could hear. A few moments later, she opened her eyes and said, "I believe Thea left on her own and Eliot followed. 'Tis what I see, but I also see Eliot with Fulke. That doesn't make sense."

"Aye, it does. Eliot followed and he got too close to Fulke. Fulke grabbed Eliot to draw Thea out." Willum looked to both and said, "Since he knew Eliot, if he'd seen him anywhere, he would have grabbed him. After all, it was Eliot's fault that Thea was freed. At least, Slater would view it that way. We have to go after them. I'm going to the stable to get my horse ready."

"I'll be there shortly. I wish to speak with Logan first," Maitland said.

Dyna joined Willum, and they headed out through the gates. "She overheard us last eve, did she no'? I thought I saw the two of ye through the trees when I left. Logan didnae see ye."

"Aye, we were on a ride when we heard the voices. We were too shocked to say anything."

"We all know how Logan is about eavesdropping, so I willnae question ye there."

"How did ye discover Thea had gone?" Willum asked. He knew Thea could be quiet as a mouse when the situation called for it.

"Maitland came out early to prepare for the patrol's departure and noticed the missing horses, then discovered Eliot and Thor were gone, too. He thought the lad might have ridden down to Thea's cottage, since he's been asking after her, so he sent a guard to fetch him back. But he was no' there, and neither was Thea."

A loud bark interrupted them, and they turned to see a dog streaking down the road toward them.

Gerland barked again then ran straight for Torrian, who'd just come out of the gate. Torrian knelt down and the animal came right to him, barking. After one lick of Torrian's hand, he dashed a few paces back the way he'd come, then paused and turned back, waiting for the human to follow.

"Ye know where she is, do ye no', Gerland? Then we'll follow ye. Here, boy. Come get some water after yer run." Torian led the dog toward the stable.

Torrian stopped next to Willum and Dyna. "Will ye come with me? Willum, I'd welcome yer sword, and Dyna yer bow and yer visions, if ye have any that will help."

Willum nodded. "Dyna and I will go with ye now, and Maitland is coming. I would go even if we didn't have Gerland to guide us."

Torrian clapped him on the shoulder. "I'll leave word for another group to join us if we dinnae return by high sun. Alaric and Eli can get the next group ready."

"We have to find her before then," Willum said, his voice trailing off.

He couldn't abide the thought of Thea alone with Fulke for any amount of time.

He dreaded finding out exactly what the man was capable of.

CHAPTER TWENTY-TWO

THEA STEPPED OUT of the woods, holding her bow in front of her. "Are ye wishing for one in the other shoulder, Slater? Let the lad go."

She should have shot him quickly. By warning him, she'd given him the opportunity to pull the lad in front of him, holding a dagger at the boy's neck.

"I do not think so. I have plans for you. You're both coming with me to the next inn. If you make a single move to run away, I'll kill him, slice his neck in front of you. At the inn, you will get me food and a healer for the wound in my leg."

Thea took the time to assess the man. He looked feverish. His eyes held that odd glaze, his hands shook, and he kept swiping at his lips. Hungry? Thirsty? If he was as hungry as many of the English were said to be, that could account for the shaking hands and the swipe at his dry lips. But the gaze was feverish. Of that much she was certain.

"Ye have the fever, Fulke. Ye'll no' get far."

"Nay, no fever," he declared, taking a swipe across his forehead.

"Aye, ye do. I can see the green discharge coming from yer leg. Ye may beat it, but mayhap ye willnae. Let the boy go. He has naught to do with this. 'Tis just ye and me." Thea had never been more certain of anything in her life. She would get this lad away from this bastard, then deal with him. Proud to say that she held no fear, she would act without hesitation, and do what had to be done. *Lorana, help me set Eliot free.*

Her father was right. She could almost feel Lorana peering over her shoulder.

"I just passed an inn not too far back. We'll go to that one. A place where I can eat and then take care of both of ye."

"Yer demands are proof ye know nothing about where ye've come. There is no inn behind us either. Did ye forget ye are no' in England? This is the edge of the Highlands and there are verra few inns here." She had to admit that her hands were sweating more than she would have liked. She hadn't been expecting to have to negotiate with the fool. And she surely hadn't expected to see Eliot with him. The lad had followed her, which squeezed her heart a wee bit, but filled her with fear, too. This was even more motivation to kill the bastard threatening both of them. She'd hoped to kill him and be done with him. If her hands weren't shaking, she'd put an arrow in his eye, but after the misses she had when her brother was involved, she knew she could not take the risk.

Once this was resolved, everyone would call her foolish, and they would be right. She shouldn't have come alone. She hadn't expected Eliot to follow her. The danger he was now in was all her fault.

"Then we head back to the inn I passed not long ago. I saw that one. If you try anything, the lad dies. This is a simple request. Food for both of your lives."

"Fine. I'll go along with ye for now." Torrian and Willum would be along soon. Gerland would bring them swiftly. All she had to do was stall for time.

She locked her gaze on Eliot's, doing her best to let him know that they would both come through this without any problem.

"You have a horse on the path? Lead me there. You'll ride in front, so I can watch you. And drop your weapons. I'll be holding the boy in front of me, and if you try anything, he dies. Understand?"

"Understood." She set her bow off to the side of the path, but somewhere she hoped they'd be seen by Torrian. She also left her dagger there too. The one in her boot stayed hidden. At least she'd had the foresight to bring it along.

She mounted her horse and led the way, thinking of ten different ways to attack the bastard, but she was dissatisfied with all her possibilities. Every tactic she could think of would put Eliot at risk, and she was not willing to do that.

There was one fact that could work in her favor. Fulke was not in good shape. She reviewed everything she knew about him so she wouldn't make any mistakes.

The wound on his leg was still open and leaking more than blood along with oozing a bit of green. She also was certain that he had a fever. His eyes were glazed, his face flushed, and his hands had a slight tremor, all signs of illness from a wound gone bad. The tremors could also be from hunger. If enough time passed, the man would collapse in front of her without her doing a thing.

The more she thought on it, the more convinced she was of his illness. And he must be starving, if he'd rather find food before taking his revenge on her. Being hungry would also make him weak. Perhaps Eliot was strong enough to fight him off.

But she did not want Eliot attempting anything. Not yet.

At this point, she had no alternative but to do what he asked. The best way was to go slowly to waste time until help arrived. She had no doubt it would be here shortly. She prayed Gerland could guide Torrian back to this spot. One other reason to go slowly popped into her head. If they made it to the inn, she'd be going inside to steal, and she could easily be caught.

The punishment for stealing from an establishment like that could be cutting off the thief's hand. She rubbed her wrist at the thought. Her second fear was that an inn's common room would largely be occupied by men, possibly a few in their cups already.

That meant wandering hands and disgusting proposals. Not that she'd be walking openly into the common room, if she were to try to steal food, but if she were caught, the consequences might be worse than losing a hand.

The only other possibility was to locate a manor home or hamlet where she could steal food. That was her plan then. Find a home that appeared to be empty. Or one she knew. They were nearly on Menzie land and Uncle Drew and Aunt Lina had friends along this path.

They'd traveled a short time in uncomfortable silence when a manor home came into view. A large number of people were milling about, though she had no idea what they were doing. There were some she could hear behind the home, so she guessed they were tending the horses tethered back there since it was still early morning.

But that also meant there would be food in the home. She just had to find a way to sneak inside, try begging for food before stealing, then bring it to Fulke. If she were lucky, someone would recognize the Ramsay plaid and would be friendly.

It was worth a try. And she wouldn't allow Fulke to dissuade her from going inside in search of food.

"I'm stopping here." She dismounted before he gave her any choice. She very deliberately did not tether her horse. She wanted to be able to get away quickly, if she had the chance.

"Nay, ye'll go on to the inn."

She never looked at him, creeping forward instead. Her voice came out in a loud whisper, "Ye and I are both starving. I canno' wait for food that may no' be there at an inn. And this will be easier than trying to steal food from a busy inn. Store rooms are rarely guarded and many of the occupants are out back. At least, men with weapons are with their horses."

She glanced over her shoulder. Poor Eliot was doing his best not to move, but she could see the dagger had already cut him once, a small line of blood now trickling down his neck.

"Come back, you bitch!"

Ignoring him, she headed straight to the home, waving Fulke back into the trees so they'd not be seen.

Nearly to the entrance, she peeked inside the partially open door, noticing a few women busying themselves over a pot in the hearth. Moving around to the side, she noticed a window open a wee bit, so she decided to try her luck.

"Good morrow to ye," she said through the window, pushing one shutter back. "I am from Ramsay land and in an unfortunate predicament. Might ye have a half loaf of bread to share?

Enough to shut Fulke up for now.

The woman looked at the other, a clear question on her face. The second one said, "She's wearing a Ramsay plaid. Drew would give her the bread. Too many are starving and we are fortunate."

The other woman broke a loaf in half and set it on a table in front of the window.

Thea said, "Many thanks to ye." She grabbed the hunk of bread and moved quietly toward the front of the house. A voice carried from the back of the house so she took off, taking cover in the trees. She waved to Fulke as she passed him by holding out the partial loaf of bread.

She feared one of the men might engage in pursuit, but nothing happened. Fulke followed her into the trees, still keeping Eliot close on his horse. As soon as she felt safe, deep enough into the forest to be hidden from view, she stopped, handing over the bread to him.

He grabbed it, his eyes looking feverish and frantic. He took such a big bite off the loaf that he could barely chew it. Drool rolled down his chin. This was her opportunity.

As soon as he took his second bite, Thea launched herself at him, knocking him off his horse, though he kept hold of the reins. Eliot tumbled to the ground, too, and scrambled out of the way of Fulke's grab and the horse's hooves. At the same time, a group of people rounded the manor home, two of them on horseback, shouting at them.

"Ye there. Leave the boy. We'll hunt ye down!"

Thea leapt onto her horse then held her hand down for Eliot. He swung up behind her with such force that he nearly fell off the opposite side. Thea grabbed him until the boy wrapped his arms around her waist. Then she kicked her horse into a run, heading away from the angry group racing toward them.

"He's English. He's the one who stole from us before," she heard, refusing to look back.

"Ye bastard. We'll no' let ye go. We can tell ye are one of the English stealing from our homes and this is no' the first time."

Thea couldn't believe her ears. Were they chasing Fulke and not the two of them? She decided to get a distance a way before stopping to check.

They zigzagged around trees, Eliot slipping and sliding a bit until he adjusted to the pace. Once they were stable, Thea glanced back over her shoulder, pleased to see the residents of the manor she'd taken the bread from had stopped Fulke, reclaiming the food he attempted to hide behind his back.

Now she only had one problem.

Where the hell were they? She had no idea which way to go. Slowing to calm her beating heart, she checked her surroundings, knowing they were not far from the main path. She just had to find her way there and head back to Ramsay land.

Suddenly, a falcon caught her eye. Blue was circling overhead.

Nothing could have made her smile more. Willum was close.

CHAPTER TWENTY-THREE

THE SEARCH PARTY stopped in the middle of a crossroad.

"Where the hell did she go?" Willum asked. Gerland had led them to a clearing where they'd found obvious signs that someone had just been camping there. And at first their trail had been obvious. Wandering horses in the woods couldn't help but show signs of their passing. But their luck hadn't lasted.

Dyna shook her head. "We have to split up. We'll never cover enough ground with us all together. We're no' far from Menzie land. They have to be close. We followed her tracks for a while, but now they've disappeared. Mayhap she is no longer on horseback."

"'Tis possible," Torrian said, glancing around the area. "This is a heavily wooded area. I doubt they are far off the path. The trees are too dense. Let's each take a different direction. Dyna go south, Maitland east, I'll go west, and Willum, go back to that fork we just passed and take the other branch. We'll meet back here in an hour."

They took off in opposite directions, and

Willum could feel the walls of panic settling around him. He didn't wish to do this. That wasn't quite true. He wished to find Thea, but not alone. But he would do what he needed to do to find her. Saving her was worth facing his fears. He whistled for his falcon, Blue not far away.

If Thea were near, she would recognize Blue and go toward him.

He headed back to the fork in the road, not encountering anyone, and continued in the opposite direction from where they had traveled initially.

He followed the path, looking on either side of the road for any signs of recent travel by animal or human. He'd learned to track from his parents long ago, and it has stood him in good stead over the years.

He saw no evidence of anyone. The forest was not quite as thick here, so he dismounted and led his horse into the woods, venturing into the unknown for any sign of dear Thea.

Being alone in the forest brought him back to a place he didn't want to be, a memory that had hung on him, tortured him for years now. How he'd tried to release himself from the horror of those three days, but it wouldn't leave him be.

The buzzing of an insect took him back as if he were six again…

———◦∞◦———

Willum chased the butterfly, laughing as it darted and changed directions so quickly that he couldn't catch it.

"Hold still so I can catch ye. I'll no' harm ye, I promise." He followed it down one path and onto another, not noticing that he'd gone a long way from where he started.

He chased it until he ran out of breath, laughing and enjoying every time he nearly caught the orange creature. To his dismay, the butterfly flew above his head and out of his reach. He watched it for a moment, then turned around to return to his parents.

"Mama?"

No one was behind him. He frowned. He'd only just left his parents a moment ago. Hadn't it been just a moment?

The worst part was the area was totally unrecognizable. Scowling, he followed his path back only for it to disappear under his feet, one of the hundreds of animal tracks in these woods rather than a real path. No matter, he could see trampled grass just ahead, and he followed that sweep of green until he hit an area of stone.

He didn't recall running across stone. He surely would have felt the small rocks under the leather of his boots, wouldn't he? Whirling again in a circle, he had no idea where he was.

Maybe they would find him? His mother was about to have a new brother or sister for him, so she did not move quickly, but his sire could come searching. He'd been close by.

Or had he? The more Willum thought, the more he wondered if he'd heard his sire say he was going hunting. He glanced over his head, looking for his father's falcons, but didn't see any.

Willum had to admit the inevitable. He was lost.

Looking up at the dropping sun, he vowed to find his way back before dark. He said a quick prayer for guidance to find his way back, because he hated the dark.

As his sire often told him when he was younger, he had to get used to it because it wasn't as though they could just turn the sun on to show their way wherever they went. He'd tried so hard to adjust to the dark but wherever he looked, something appeared.

A wolf in the back of the cave.

Bats above his head.

Monsters under the bed that he slept in when they stayed in the Ramsay keep.

The meanest, ugliest reiver he'd ever seen behind the trees.

He walked and walked and walked, calling out to his parents all along the way, but got no response from anyone. Midges covered him. He swatted at them but they wouldn't stop.

He needed that fine net his mother had made for him to sleep under in the worst of the summer.

He swatted and killed bug after bug, cursing at each one. He scratched until he screamed, leaning his head back and screaming as loud as he could, praying his mother would hear him.

Instead, a bug flew into his mouth.

He cried and cried and cried.

Willum shook his head to send the memories away. He had to get control of his mind and focus. Thea needed him. He vowed to rid himself of his childish fears. Taking a deep breath, he continued into the thick of the woods but didn't see any sign of anyone. He turned around to go back, but he caught a flash of color out of the corner of his eye. Up ahead, there was a piece of clothing caught on a bush.

A piece of Ramsay plaid. True, it could have been anyone's, but he had to consider the possibility that it came from Eliot or Thea. He brushed his fingers across it, then searched the ground for any sign of footprints or horse hooves.

Hope developed in a moment. Off to the side of the main path, he found her weapons. One bow and the dagger she carried were tossed off to the side of the path. This had to be where she came upon Fulke and Eliot.

He found true evidence of them. Two horses and three people. Exactly what he was looking for. Hope blossomed inside him, and even though his memories still assailed him, the hope made them easier to ignore. He wasn't going to let them prevent him from finding Thea and Eliot.

He retrieved his horse and followed the trail, vowing to focus on what was important—Eliot and Thea.

He loved her with all his heart, with all his soul. When they were apart, he felt as if a part of him was missing. If he didn't find her…

His sweaty palm stuck to his horse's reins, but he ignored it, wishing it away the same way he did the sweat running down his back. He ignored the pull of his memory and focused on Thea. Where did they go?

The trail he followed paralleled the path, so he left the trees so he could move more quickly. He watched for evidence that they'd changed direction, but saw nothing. A quarter of an hour passed, and he was about to return to their meeting place when he heard a commotion up ahead.

A group of Scots dragged a man across the path, trying to take something from his hands. Willum would swear it was Fulke Slater. Hoping for a better look, he approached the group, slowing his mount. It was indeed Fulke and he fought with the strength that only comes from desperation to hang on to what looked like a partial loaf of bread, managing to hold off four men. He cursed and yelled like he was daft, and when Willum noticed that his trousers were wet where Dyna's arrow had struck him days ago, he realized the man was probably daft with fever.

At the sound of a falcon's screeching cry, Willum looked up, pleased to see Blue soaring above him. Before he could whistle to the bird, a group of reivers burst out of the woods, four on horseback and two running.

He thought they were headed toward the melee, but it soon became clear they were heading directly at him. He stared at the fools in disbelief. Was one man really worth risking injury or death? Because although the numbers were not in his favor, his sword was.

"Get his horse!"

Now that he knew exactly what they were after, he decided it was time to fight back. He whistled for Blue, calling him down. Then he unsheathed his sword. The fools came at him with only daggers barely large enough to be worthy of the word.

He cut two down before Blue flew into the middle of the madness, his talons catching one man's face and sending him running for the shelter of the woods. That left three men on horseback.

Blue outsmarted all of them. He flew near one horse's face, and the animal reared, tossing its rider, and spooking the other two horses into running the other way. The man on the ground scrambled after them.

Willum didn't expect them to come back, so he turned back to the fight between Fulke and the other men. The four—presumably from the nearby house—had retrieved their stolen goods and were nearly back to their door.

Fulke was staggering away down the path. Willum put his sword back in its sheath and took out his bow, nocking an arrow and taking aim.

"He's mine, Willum. Dinnae shoot him."

Willum lowered his bow and looked to where the voice had come from. Thea's voice. And there she was, his beautiful avenging angel, sitting on one of the Ramsay war horses, just emerging from the woods to his right.

"Bitch!" Fulke yelled over his shoulder. Willum figured that he'd heard Thea's voice, though he scanned the area looking for her. Not being able to see her didn't stop him from shouting louder, "You'll suck me off before I choke the breath out of you."

He lurched into a halting run, a wild screech ripping through the air.

Willum touched his heels to his horse's flanks to follow the bastard, and Thea did the same. A wild smile broke out on Willum's face. Coming behind Thea was his group, Torrian, Maitland, and Dyna.

Fulke saw her then, and took up his screaming again. "I'm going to kill you!" He ran straight toward her with a roar, his dagger over his head.

Thea kneed her horse to slow, then stood in the stirrups, bowstring to her ear. Her arrow hit him in the chest before he took two more steps. He collapsed to the ground and didn't move.

Willum had to see her up close with his own eyes. While the others dismounted to check Fulke, he headed straight for Thea, sliding out of the saddle only when he was next to her.

Thea covered her mouth with her hand to muffle the sobs erupting from her. Willum reached for her waist, lifted her carefully off the horse and embraced her in a tight hug.

"I love ye, Thea. I hope ye will be mine forever."

Thea nodded and clung to him, soaking his tunic with her tears.

She was safe. Finally.

CHAPTER TWENTY-FOUR

THEA AND THE rest crossed onto Ramsay land later that same day. She was anxious to see her sire, but also wasn't sure she quite wanted the journey to end. She rode with Willum and quite liked being tucked against him, his heat warming her. When she was finally able to control her sobs, she whispered, "I love ye too, Willum."

He reached down to squeeze her hand and kissed the top of her head. "Does that mean if I propose to ye, ye would accept?" Before she could answer, he squeezed her hand again and said, "Nay. 'Tis the wrong way to do it." He stopped his horse for a moment and turned her to face him. "Thea, will ye marry me? We dinnae have to marry right away. I can wait until ye are ready and wait until yer sire is hale again. Or if…"

Her finger came up to his lips to stop him. "Aye. I accept. And we have time to decide when we will marry. Dinnae worry about that now."

He kissed her thoroughly, teasing shouts coming from the people on horseback around the two of them.

"Watch out, here comes Uncle Logan," Dyna said.

Willum pulled back to glance over his shoulder, and the surrounding group laughed.

"Teasing ye," Dyna said just as she spurred her horse forward.

Thea arranged herself facing forward again. "I need to see Papa before I do anything else." She laced her fingers with Willum's, squeezing his hand as they continued.

Slater was gone and she was betrothed to Willum. Of course, she would have to get her parents' approval, but she already knew her sire liked Willum and would agree to the match. He'd told her so only…only the day before. Had it been so recent? Too much had happened since then.

They approached the cottage, and Thea was pleased to see her sire sitting on a bench in the sun. He'd built it himself so visitors had a place to sit when the day was pleasant. To see him sitting there, looking as good as ever, pleased her more than she could ever admit.

"Papa," she called out. "Are ye hale? No more problems?"

He smiled and waved to her, getting up once they were close enough for her to dismount. She hurried over to his side, wrapping her arms around him. "Ye are hale? Where is Mama? Willum asked me to marry him and Slater is dead."

"Slow down, daughter. One thing at a time. I am fine. Mama has gone to the keep because Torrian's dog is having trouble delivering her litter. I'm glad Slater is no more a threat to ye, but the other item ye mentioned is what I wish to hear more on. Willum asked ye to marry him, and what was yer answer?"

"Aye. Of course, I said aye. I love him with all my heart." She giggled as she began to form her words to explain exactly what Willum meant to her, but Eliot interrupted them.

"Thea! Help me!" Tears streamed down his face as he approached their cottage on horseback, carrying Thor across the saddle in front of him. "I didnae know where he went, so I went looking for him. I found him on the side of the road. Can ye fix him, Thea? Please?"

"What happened to him? Poor Thor. Willum, will ye go ask Mama to come back? She can help him."

Her father stood behind her and moved his hands to her shoulders. "Thea, yer mother is busy, and this dog doesnae have much time left. She has trained ye to help her. Ye will have to do what ye can. Willum will pass the message on, but it could be too late for this animal. It's up to ye to save him."

She whirled around to stare at her father, wide-eyed. "Me? I canno'…"

"Aye, ye can. I've seen ye work with yer Mama many times. Ye know what to do and ye are talented. I'll carry him into Mama's shed. Get whatever tools ye may need. Ye are more than capable."

Willum moved over to her side and whispered in her ear. "I was in the woods alone looking for ye, and I got past my fears. 'Tis time for ye to get past yer own fears. All of them." He kissed her cheek, then mounted and galloped off with a wave. Donnan took Thor from Eliot, then the boy slid to the ground.

"Come along with us, lad. We may need yer help." Donnan led the way, leaving Thea no choice. She had to do what she could for poor Thor.

Eliot's tears slowed but didn't stop. Thea had to ignore his distress. The pressure of possibly making a mistake that could cause Eliot to lose his dear pet was nearly more than she could handle.

"Please help Thor, Thea. He tried to protect me."

She forced her fears back and said, "Do ye know what happened to him?"

"Nay. When Slater grabbed me, Thor tried to bite him, but he kicked him and Thor backed off. He followed for a while, but I think he may have gotten into a fight with an animal. I couldnae see him."

Donnan set him down on the tall table covered with an old blanket. Thor's eyes were closed but he'd bled heavily from a wound near his belly. Thea used a wet cloth to wash the blood away so she could see where the injury was. She found teeth marks in his side, and one spot was still bleeding heavily.

"Eliot, he's lost quite a bit of blood. If he's lost too much, it might be too late for him. But that's one reason he seems to be sleeping. Losing blood will make ye tired. I'll sew him up, and hopefully he won't awaken until after that. Then we must get him to eat and drink to make up for all he's lost."

"I'll do whatever ye need, my lady." The hope in the boy's gaze humbled her. "I believe ye can fix him. Ye fixed Freya."

Her father stood across from her. "Eliot, if ye see him open his eyes while she's stitching him, please remember we must keep him from biting her. He might be startled and bite the first thing he sees. Be aware and alert."

Eliot nodded. "Aye, my lord."

"Call me Donnan, lad. Ye saved my daughter. I dinnae need formal titles in my home."

Eliot nodded.

Thea worked diligently, sewing up all the spots that were open on his belly. She managed to get the worst one first, and Thor didn't awaken. She knew this was not a good sign.

"Papa, have we any beef broth? He'll probably no' drink water, but if we can get the broth inside him, that will help."

"Aye, I'll take some from the pot over the hearth. Mama was making a stew for this eve. 'Tis no' thickened yet, so I think 'twill work for ye. Eliot, ye must watch carefully while I'm gone."

Her father quickly fetched a bowl of broth.

"I think I'm finished, Papa. We'll see if he awakens. Mama has some potion for the soreness. I'll find it."

She washed her hands, then turned back around, and was surprised to see Thor's head raised. When he saw Eliot, his tail began to wag, thumping against the work table.

"He's awake. Ye saved him, Thea," Eliot cried.

"No' yet. We need to get him to eat and drink first." She positioned the dog so he could lap up the broth, and he drank it up quickly.

As soon as he was able, he stood, though he sat back down immediately. Then he forced himself back on his feet.

"A very good sign indeed," Thea said. "We'll set him down. If ye like, Eliot, ye may sit on the floor, and he'll probably settle on yer lap."

"Before ye do that," a voice called out from behind her, "please allow me to admire yer handiwork, Thea." Her mother stood behind her with a smile, holding a wee puppy in her arms.

"Mama? A puppy?" Thea was shocked to see her mother holding a brand new puppy, his eyes still closed and his fur damp. He must have been from Torrian's litter.

"His mother doesn't wish to feed him so I've decided to take it on. I brought some goat's milk to feed the wee pup. Mayhap Eliot will hold him for me while I check yer work."

Eliot giggled when she set the pup in his arms, a plaid underneath him. "He's so little. I've no' seen one this young before."

Her mother spoke softly to Thor as she approached him, and he licked her hand as if to give her permission. "Thea, yer stitches are better than mine. Well done. Donnan, I think we'll get him another bowl of broth."

Thea stood back watching all that took place. Willum came in behind her mother, and he too began to fuss over Thor.

She'd done it. And she was proud of what she'd done. Her sire gave the next bowl to Thor, and then he clasped her shoulder.

"Well done, Thea. Ye saved Thor's life, I believe. And just as good as yer mother would

have done."

"I did, did I no'?"

"Aye, and I think ye have proven yer own words wrong."

She gave him a puzzled look. "My words?"

"Ye recall when ye told me ye were nothing special? Ye've surely proven those words to be false. Ye are indeed something special."

She blushed and hugged her father. "I'm so happy ye are up and about, Da." Her father's words were often words to cherish and remember. She was not ready to lose him yet.

"Thank ye, Thea." Eliot looked up at her as if she were the queen of Scotland.

A strange sense of satisfaction filled her, and she had the sudden realization as to what she wished to do with her life. "Mama, will ye continue to teach me so I can be yer assistant?"

"Naught would please me more." Her mother hugged her and said, "And we approve of Willum. He asked me for my approval along the way."

Her heart could take no more happiness. If anything else happened, it would surely burst open. She was in love and happy.

EPILOGUE

TORRIAN STEPPED INTO the great hall and stopped, waiting for everyone to give him their attention. The hall was full for the midday meal, but he clearly had an important announcement to make.

"Hush," Eliot said to his new friend, Perrin, who sat next to Lorna.

Lorna had settled in quite well with Liliana and her twin lasses, who were now three summers old. She spent much of her time playing with the wee ones and helping wash all the clothes they wore. She'd told Thea that it was much better than hiding away in a cellar and far better than the orphanage she'd been in.

When the hall was finally quiet, Torrian motioned to him.

"Me?" Eliot pointed to himself because he couldn't believe the chief of Clan Ramsay was calling him forward.

Torrian smiled and said, "Aye, Eliot. I'd like to speak with ye here."

Eliot got up and walked up to stand in front of Torrian. "Aye, my laird."

Torrian turned him around to face the group, his arm around Eliot's shoulders. "I'd like everyone to know that because of his dedication to keeping my niece safe, I have decided that Eliot deserves to have his own chamber inside the keep. 'Tis a small chamber, but he's earned the right to sleep inside where he can stay warm in the winter. I'm also making him my assistant kennel master. We have one new litter and another one coming soon, so I'm going to need his help taking care of the new pups. And of course, Eliot will get his pick to keep as his own pet."

The entire hall burst into applause, and Eliot blushed and then peered up at his chieftain. "Truly?" he whispered. "My own chamber?"

"Aye. Ye have earned it. Ye saved one of my precious nieces twice, and without ye, we know no' what would have happened. Yer chamber doesnae have a hearth, but heated stones at the base of yer bed will keep ye warm enough. Ye'll have plenty of plaids to pile on yer bed, too. Do ye accept yer new position, lad?"

"Aye, sir," Eliot said.

"I'll take ye there in a few moments. Now go finish yer meal."

Willum congratulated Eliot, but stopped in his tracks because he noticed Uncle Logan motioning for Dyna and Maitland to join him in the solar. Willum moved over, stepping in behind Dyna, hoping he'd be permitted to hear the latest news.

Logan waved them all inside, including Thea when she appeared in the doorway. "Fine, fine. I'll tell ye all what I just learned from the messenger."

"Go on," Maitland said. "I dinnae think this is good news."

"'Tis no'. Ye are wanted by King Robert again. Douglas is doing his best to protect the Borderlands from the English, but they continue to cause trouble. He was told that a large group left Berwick Castle looking for provisions. Edward has no' sent any rations, and they are all starving. Their plan is to find a cattle farm to raid and take as many beasts as possible back to Berwick. We canno' allow that to happen."

"So he wishes for our help?" Maitland asked.

"Aye. He wants ye to search the area. Find those men before they raid one of the estates. He wishes for ye to leave on the morrow. No delays. Sir James Douglas is counting on our assistance. Choose yer team."

Maitland turned to Willum and Thea. "Do ye wish to join us?"

Willum glanced at Thea who nodded her head. "Aye, we'll be there."

"We'll take four more. Alaric, Eli, Tevis and Wenna. I want eight on this trip."

"Prepare for battle. It will be a big one," Dyna said, fixing her plait. "I saw it in my dream last eve."

THE END

www.keiramontclair.com

DEAR READER,
    Thank you for reading Thea and Willum's story. The next book I am working on is the last book in the series and centers around Elisant Ramsay, Gavin and Merewen's youngest daughter, and Alaric Grant, Jamie and Gracie's younger son.

This story will bring us to the Battle of Skaithmur, a true battle that gave Sir James Douglas his nickname, the Black Douglas. You will meet him in the story. The battle actually takes place in the winter, but I moved it forward a couple of months later since this is fiction. I do play with history a bit. Yes, I admit it.

This last book will tie the two clans together again, just like the second book did with Brenna Grant and Quade Ramsay. This series is the third generation of the Ramsay, as Highland Swords is the third generation of the Grants. However, Logan Ramsay will not die at the end of this book.

But he is a prominent character throughout this story. It's not finished yet, but a work in progress.

That will be book 8, the last of this series. I'm hoping my muse comes up with a Christmas novella for book 9, but nothing certain yet.

Happy reading!

Keira Montclair
www.keiramontclair.com

Novels by Keira Montclair

HIGHLAND HUNTERS
THE SCOT'S CONFLICT
THE SCOT'S TRAITOR
THE SCOT'S PROTECTOR
THE SCOT'S VOW
THE SCOT'S DESTINY
THE SCOT'S WARNING
THE SCOT'S RECKONING

THE SOULMATE CHRONICLES
#1 TRUSTING A HIGHLANDER
#2 TRUSTING A SCOT
#3 TRUSTING A CHIEFTAIN

STAND-ALONE BOOKS
ESCAPE TO THE HIGHLANDS
THE BANISHED HIGHLANDER
REFORMING THE DUKE-REGENCY
WOLF AND THE WILD SCOTS
FALLING FOR THE CHIEFTAIN-3RD in a
collaborative trilogy
HIGHLAND SECRETS -3rd in a collaborative
trilogy

THE SUMMERHILL SERIES-
CONTEMPORARY ROMANCE
#1-ONE SUMMERHILL DAY
#2-A FRESH START FOR TWO
#3-THREE REASONS TO LOVE

ABOUT THE AUTHOR

KEIRA MONTCLAIR IS the pen name of an author who lives in South Carolina with her husband. She loves to write fast-paced, emotional romance, especially with children as secondary characters.

When she's not writing, she loves to spend time with her grandchildren. She's worked as a high school math teacher, a registered nurse, and an office manager. She loves ballet, mathematics, puzzles, learning anything new, and creating new characters for her readers to fall in love with.

She writes historical romantic suspense. Her bestselling series is a family saga that follows two medieval Scottish clans through three generations and now numbers over forty books.

Contact her through her website:
www.keiramontclair.com